Lost and Found

A Samantha Classic
Volume 2

by Valerie Tripp

★ American Girl®

Published by American Girl Publishing
Copyright © 1987, 1998, 2014 American Girl

Questions or comments? Call 1-800-845-0005, visit **americangirl.com**,
or write to Customer Service, American Girl,
8400 Fairway Place, Middleton, WI 53562.

Printed in China
14 15 16 17 18 19 20 LEO 10 9 8 7 6 5 4 3 2 1

This book is a work of fiction. Any similarity to real persons, living or dead,
is coincidental and not intended by American Girl. References to real events,
people, or places are used fictitiously. Other names, characters, places, and
incidents are the products of imagination.

Cover image by Michael Dwornik and Juliana Kolesova

Cataloging-in-Publication Data available from the Library of Congress

To Christopher Wallace Draper,
Charlotte Kathleen Campbell,
Patrick Granger Campbell, and
the Petty, Heuer, and Dalton Families

Beforever

Beforever is about making connections. It's about exploring the past, finding your place in the present, and thinking about the possibilities your future can bring. And it's about seeing the common thread that ties girls from all times together. The inspiring characters you will meet stand up for what they care about most: Helping others. Protecting the earth. Overcoming injustice. Through their courageous stories, discover how staying true to your own beliefs will help make your world better today—and tomorrow.

TABLE *of* CONTENTS

1	Petticoats and Petit Fours	1
2	The Party	10
3	New York City	22
4	Follow That Dog!	31
5	Changes	39
6	Piney Point	47
7	The Sketchbook	61
8	Teardrop Island	71
9	Through the Passage	85
10	A New Home	96
11	Searching for Nellie	105
12	Coldrock House	116
13	In the Alley	127
14	Together	137
	Inside Samantha's World	148

Petticoats and Petit Fours

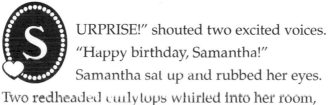

CHAPTER 1

"URPRISE!" shouted two excited voices. "Happy birthday, Samantha!"

Samantha sat up and rubbed her eyes. Two redheaded curlytops whirled into her room, jumped up on her bed, and pushed a huge bouquet of roses into her arms. "This is for you!" said the redhead named Agnes.

"Jiminy!" exclaimed Samantha. "It's beautiful!"

"We made it ourselves," added Agatha proudly. Agatha looked exactly like Agnes. They were Aunt Cornelia's twin sisters. Now that Uncle Gard and Cornelia were married, Agnes and Agatha were Samantha's newest friends and favorite relatives.

Samantha put her nose deep into the roses. "No one ever gave me flowers for my birthday before," she said.

"I knew you'd like them," said Agnes happily. "It was my idea to give you a bouquet."

"Well, it was my idea to wrap the stems in lace," insisted Agatha.

Samantha looked at the bottom of the bouquet. "Where did you get all this nice lace?" she asked. "It looks sort of like it came off a petticoat."

The twins looked at each other and giggled.

"Did you cut up your petticoat?" Samantha asked.

"Not exactly," said Agatha. She leaned back and twisted one of her red curls around her finger. "There was already a rip where the ruffle was attached. We just sort of helped the rip get bigger until the ruffle fell off."

"Gosh!" said Samantha. "Grandmary would be furious if I cut up one of my petticoats. Won't your mother be angry?"

"Oh, no," said Agnes lightly. "That petticoat was getting too small for us anyway."

"Besides," said Agatha, "our mother is used to us and our ideas by now."

Samantha laughed out loud. Sometimes it seemed to her that Agnes's and Agatha's ideas spilled out all over the place, like popcorn popping out of a pot. During the week of their visit, the twins had turned Grandmary's quiet house in Mount Bedford topsy-turvy. Samantha liked it that way.

Agnes sprawled on Samantha's bed, swinging her legs over the side. "Hurry and get dressed," she said. "We smelled something absolutely scrumptious coming from the kitchen."

"Ooooh! I bet Mrs. Hawkins is making a birthday treat for breakfast!" said Samantha as she scrambled out of bed. "I'll be dressed in a jiffy." She pulled her long underwear out of the drawer.

"Oh, don't bother with that," said Agnes. "No one wears long underwear anymore." Agnes and Agatha were from New York City, so they knew all about the latest fashions.

"I *have* to," sighed Samantha. "It's one of Grandmary's rules: long underwear from September to the end of June." She pulled the underwear onto one leg.

"Jeepers!" exclaimed Agatha. "What an old-fashioned rule! You'll roast if you wear that today."

Samantha held out her leg and looked at the underwear. "I do hate it," she said.

"Then don't wear it," said Agnes simply. "Make up your own mind for once."

Samantha sat up very straight. "I'm ten years old today," she said. "I guess that's old enough to think for myself about things like underwear." She peeled off the itchy underwear, rolled it up into a ball, and shoved it to the back of the dresser drawer. When she pulled her stockings on over her bare legs, she felt deliciously light and free.

"Come on," she said to the twins as she buttoned up her dress. "Let's go have breakfast." She grabbed her bouquet off the bed. "I can't wait to show these roses to Hawkins."

"Hawkins has already seen them," said Agatha as the girls trotted down the hall. "They're from his bush."

Samantha stopped still. "Uh-oh," she said. "No one is allowed to touch Hawkins's special rosebush!"

"Don't worry," laughed Agnes. "There were millions of roses on that bush. Hawkins won't mind that we borrowed a few."

And to Samantha's surprise, Agnes was right. Hawkins didn't mind about the roses. "What a

lovely birthday surprise!" he said. His eyes twinkled.
"Mrs. Hawkins and I have a birthday surprise for you,
too, Miss Samantha." He pushed open the kitchen door,
and there was Mrs. Hawkins with a plate of blueberry
muffins. One of the muffins had a candle stuck right in
the middle.

"Oooh!" exclaimed Samantha. "Blueberry muffins!"

"Make a wish!" said Agatha. "Blow out the candle."

"That's easy," laughed Samantha. She scrunched
her eyes shut and wished that being ten would be
completely different from being nine. She was ready
for some changes. Then she blew the candle out with
one puff.

As the twins clapped, Mrs. Hawkins said, "Well,
that *was* easy. But this afternoon, you'll have a cake
with ten candles. You'll surely have to huff and puff
then, love."

Agatha bounced on her chair. "I have a wonderful
idea, Mrs. Hawkins!" she exclaimed. "Instead of one
cake with ten candles, you could make ten little cakes
and put a candle on each one of them!"

"Ten cakes?" asked Mrs. Hawkins. She sounded
doubtful.

"Ten little teeny-tiny cakes," said Agatha. "They're called petit fours. Ladies have them at all the fancy tea parties in New York."

"Petit fours," Samantha repeated. "They sound so elegant. Could you try to make them, Mrs. Hawkins? Please?"

"Well, I don't know," said Mrs. Hawkins slowly. "We never had anything so different before."

"That's why it's such a wonderful idea," pleaded Samantha. "No one in Mount Bedford has ever had ten cakes. All the girls will be so surprised."

Mrs. Hawkins smiled at Samantha. "If you want ten cakes, you shall have them, love," she said. "I guess I can try something new."

"I have an idea for something new, too," Agnes piped up. "What if you shaped each girl's ice cream in a little ice cream mold? That's how they do it at the big ice cream parlors in the city."

Samantha was very excited. The twins had such good ideas! "Could we change the ice cream, too?" she asked Hawkins. "Except I still want it to be peppermint. That's my absolute favorite kind."

Hawkins laughed. "We can change the shape of the

ice cream without changing the flavor," he said. "As soon as I've washed the ice cream freezer, you may help me make it."

"Meanwhile, you chickadees scoot outside," said Mrs. Hawkins, rolling up her sleeves. "I don't want you underfoot while I'm making your petit fours."

Samantha and the twins finished their blueberry muffins and hurried outside into the sunshine. The trees were covered with shiny green leaves, as if they'd decorated themselves in honor of Samantha's birthday. Samantha was telling the twins how ice cream was made when a voice behind them said, "Hey, carrot heads."

It was Eddie Ryland, Samantha's pesky next-door neighbor.

Agnes scowled at him. "Don't say 'hey,'" she said. "Hay is for horses."

"You ought to know," said Eddie. "You eat like a horse."

The girls rolled their eyes at each other while Eddie laughed at his own joke. "So, what are you ninnies doing today?" he went on.

"Nothing," said all three girls quickly.

But just at that moment, Hawkins appeared with the freezer.

"I know! You're making ice cream!" said Eddie. "I know *everything* about ice cream. I'll help."

"No!" said the girls in one voice.

"You just go away, Eddie," Agatha ordered.

"Who's going to make me?" Eddie challenged.

"*I'll* make you," Agatha began. Samantha saw that Agatha was making a fist. She knew Agatha would punch Eddie right in the nose if she wanted to. Not even Grandmary's strictest rule—GIRLS DON'T FIGHT—would stop Agatha once she was mad.

"Oh, all right, Eddie," Samantha said quickly. "You can help us make ice cream, but don't be a pest." She whispered to the twins, "Just ignore him. Maybe he'll go away."

The girls and Eddie watched as Hawkins poured ice chips into the ice cream freezer. "Now it's time to add the salt," said Samantha. She scooped up handfuls of rock salt from a sack and poured the salt on the ice.

"Use just enough to keep the ice melted," warned Hawkins.

"And keep it away from the lid of the container,"

Eddie added in a know-it-all voice. "Because if any salt gets inside, the ice cream will be ruined."

"We don't need you to boss us, Eddie," said Agatha. She pushed her shoulder in front of Eddie to block his view.

"This ice cream is going to be the best ice cream anyone ever ate," Samantha said happily as Hawkins began turning the crank of the freezer.

"I can't wait to taste it," said Agnes.

"Me, either," said Samantha.

"Me, either," said Agatha.

"Me, either," said Eddie. But the girls just ignored him.

The Party

 amantha was tying a big bow in the sash of her pinafore when Grandmary came into her room. "Happy birthday, dear," she said. "I have something special for you to wear at your party. Turn and face the mirror."

Samantha was very still while Grandmary stood behind her and fastened an old-fashioned circlet of silk rosebuds in her hair. "Oh, Grandmary," Samantha sighed. "It's lovely."

Grandmary smiled. "Your mother wore this circlet at her tenth birthday party. I'm sure she would have been happy to see it passed on to you now. You look just as pretty as she did."

"Thank you very much," Samantha said.

"You are welcome, my dear," said Grandmary. "Now let's go down and wait for your guests.

It's almost time for them to arrive."

Samantha felt fluttery with excitement as she stood
in front of the house next to Grandmary. She couldn't
wait until her friends saw the wonderful surprises she
and the twins had planned for them. One by one the
girls came up the walk, dressed in their very best
party dresses. Each girl carried her favorite doll in
one arm and a brightly wrapped present for Samantha
in the other. Even though Samantha knew everyone
well, she felt a little shy as her friends said hello and
curtsied to her and to Grandmary. The guests were
shy, too, especially when they saw Agnes and Agatha.
The twins looked very grown-up in their blue party
dresses, which were the latest style from New York.

The girls sat quietly in a circle of wicker chairs on
the sunny side lawn. They sat up straight, their legs
crossed at the ankles. Their dolls sat up straight, too,
and stared at each other across the circle. Samantha
tried to begin a polite, grown-up conversation. "Well,"
she said at last. "It certainly is a nice day."

"Yes!" everyone agreed. Then all the girls were
quiet again. A breeze ruffled their big hairbows and
the skirts of their dresses. It looked as if a flock of

pale butterflies was fluttering rather nervously over the smooth green grass.

No one seemed to have anything to say, so Samantha tried again. "It is quite warm though—"

"Why don't you open your gifts?" Agnes interrupted.

"Good idea," murmured the rest of the girls. One by one they stepped forward and handed Samantha their presents. Everyone oohed and aahed politely as she opened a box of colored pencils from Ida, a fan from Ruth, and a big book of piano exercises from Edith Eddleton. Agnes and Agatha kept their present for last. They giggled as they came forward together and handed Samantha a big square box.

Samantha lifted the lid and held up a stout, cheerful-looking stuffed bear. Everyone squealed with delight. "A teddy bear!" exclaimed Samantha. "I love it!" She gave the bear a big hug.

"Teddy bears are the newest thing in New York," said Agnes, beaming. "We wanted you to have one of your very own."

"Thank you both!" said Samantha.

"Oh, may I hold him?" asked Ida. "He's so cute."

The friendly bear was passed from girl to girl. But after he had gone around the circle, the party got too quiet again. Everyone was trying so hard to be polite and grown-up, they were as stiff as the lace on their collars.

Samantha was relieved when a car came roaring up the drive with an ear-splitting *ooh-wah ooh-wah*! "Uncle Gard! Aunt Cornelia!" she exclaimed. Her guests bounced out of their chairs. "Hello! Hello!" they called as they followed Samantha over to the car.

Uncle Gard came straight to Samantha without even stopping to take off his driving goggles. He lifted her up into the air. "Happy samday, Bertha!" he said. All the girls giggled and Uncle Gard pretended to be confused. "Wait a minute. That's not right," he said. "I'll have to do that over." He lifted Samantha up again, gave her a kiss, and said, "Happy birthday, Samantha!"

"Oh, Gard!" laughed Aunt Cornelia. She leaned over and gave Samantha a soft kiss. "Happy, happy birthday, Samantha," she said. "There's someone I'd like you to meet." Aunt Cornelia reached into the car and lifted out a little brown and white puppy. "This is Jip, the newest member of our family," she explained.

When Samantha took Jip in her arms, he reached up and licked her chin with his warm, rough tongue. "He's perfect," Samantha sighed.

"Put him down," said Agatha, "and I'll make him do his tricks."

"Remember to keep an eye on him," warned Cornelia as Samantha carried Jip over to the side lawn. "He's frisky and he likes to run."

Samantha put Jip on the grass inside the circle of chairs. "Sit, Jip," commanded Agatha. Jip wagged his tail, but he didn't sit. "He doesn't always do what you ask him to," Agatha admitted. "Sit, Jip!" she commanded again. But Jip ignored her. He began to run wildly around the circle of girls, barking at their feet.

"He likes shoes," explained Agnes. So all the girls sat in their chairs and danced their feet up and down in front of Jip. Jip ran from girl to girl, growling and jumping at their shoes and having a wonderful time. Then Agatha's foot knocked over a box, and the teddy bear tumbled out. To the girls' delight, Jip began to growl at the bear.

"Look at Jip!" laughed Agatha. "He's acting like a

ferocious lion." She picked up the bear and waggled it
in front of Jip's face. "Grr!" she growled. "Come and get
me, Jip!"

Jip leaped up and yanked the bear out of Agatha's
hands, then scampered across the lawn, dragging the
bear by its leg. "Jip!" called Samantha. "Stop!"

"Let's go get him!" yelled Agatha. Agnes knocked
over her chair in her hurry to get up. All the girls
squealed with glee. They jumped out of their chairs
and ran after Jip and the twins.

Jip led the girls to the back of the house, in dizzy
circles around the oak tree, across the drive, through
the lilac hedge, and into the Rylands' yard. Finally, they
caught up with him next to the Rylands' birdbath.

"Grab him!" yelled Agatha. She started to take a
running leap.

"No, stop!" said Samantha. "I've got a better idea."
She took off her shoe and dangled it in front of Jip.
"Here, Jip," she called in a friendly voice.

Jip perked up his ears. "Come and get the shoe,
Jip," Samantha said. And sure enough, Jip dropped the
teddy bear, trotted over to Samantha, and grabbed the
shoe in his mouth. Samantha quickly picked him up.

His paws left muddy polka dots on her lacy pinafore.

"Hurray!" cheered the girls.

"But where's the bear?" asked Edith Eddleton.

"I have it," someone said in a bragging voice. And there was Eddie, holding Samantha's teddy bear by its nose.

"Eddie Ryland, you give me that teddy bear," ordered Samantha.

"No!" said Eddie. "Not unless you let me play with that dog." He pointed at Jip. "And I want some ice cream, too. I helped make it."

"You can't play with Jip because he belongs to my Aunt Cornelia," Samantha said firmly. "And you can't have any ice cream because it's for my party."

"And *you* are not invited," said Agatha.

Agnes agreed. "This party is only for girls."

"No boys are allowed," said Agatha. "Isn't that right, girls?"

Everyone chimed in, "Right! No boys are allowed."

"Then I'll keep the bear," said Eddie stubbornly.

"Eddie, you are a nincompoop!" said Agnes.

"Nincompoop!" said all the girls, laughing. It tickled their mouths to say such a funny word. "Eddie

is a nincompoop! Eddie is a nincompoop!" they
taunted. But before they could say "nincompoop"
again, Agatha tackled Eddie around the knees and
knocked him to the ground. She ripped the bear out
of his hands and ran back through the hedge, with all
the girls clapping and cheering behind her in a wild
stampede.

The stampede stopped short at the circle of chairs.
There stood Grandmary, waiting. "My heavens!" said
Grandmary. "Whatever has happened?"

"Oh, Grandmary," panted Samantha. "Jip ran off
with the teddy bear and we had to chase him." She
didn't mention the part about tackling Eddie, since
she *knew* that was breaking Grandmary's rule about
fighting.

"I see," said Grandmary. "Well, I hope you weren't
making a spectacle of yourselves." She looked around
at the out-of-breath girls. Agnes's sash was untied.
Agatha had grass stains on her stockings. Samantha's
circlet of roses was tilted over one ear, like a halo
gone wrong. Ida Dean had lost her hairbow entirely.
Grandmary looked almost as if she might smile, but
she didn't. Instead, she said, "You ladies seem to be a

bit warm from your exercise. Perhaps this is the perfect
time to have a cooling drink of lemonade."

Grandmary led the girls up the stairs of the porch
to the birthday table. It was set with a beautiful lace
cloth, Grandmary's best gold spoons, and a big crystal
pitcher of pink lemonade. There was a little nosegay
of pink roses at each place. After they sat down,
Samantha gave each girl a favor—a lovely lace fan.

The girls tried to act like young ladies again,
opening and closing their fans and fluttering them
elegantly in front of their faces. They nibbled on thin
tea sandwiches and sipped daintily from their goblets
of lemonade. When Mrs. Hawkins carried out the tray
of ten tiny cakes all glowing with candles, the girls
gasped with delight. Everyone sang "Happy Birthday
to You" and clapped politely when Samantha blew out
all the candles in one whoosh.

"This is such an elegant party," said Agnes as
Mrs. Hawkins put one of the petit fours on her plate.

"Would you care for some ice cream?" Samantha
asked in her most grown-up voice as Hawkins began
serving.

"Oh! Molded ice cream!" chirped Ruth. "It looks

just like it does in a fancy ice cream parlor!"

"And wait 'til you taste it!" exclaimed Agnes.

All the girls put rather large, unladylike spoonfuls in their mouths. Their faces turned as pink as the ice cream.

"Ugh!"

"Eew!"

"Ick!"

"Awful!"

The girls coughed and choked. They spat the ice cream out into their napkins. They slurped down gulps of lemonade. They clutched their throats and stuck out their tongues. They sputtered and gasped and gagged.

"SALT!" said Samantha. "This ice cream is full of salt!"

Hawkins looked puzzled. "But just a few minutes ago young Master Eddie tasted it, and he didn't complain."

"Was Eddie alone with the ice cream?" asked Samantha.

"Why, yes, I suppose he was," answered Hawkins. "Just before I put it into the molds."

"That rotten Eddie!" exclaimed Agnes. "He put

salt in the ice cream and ruined it for all of us!"

"Where is he? I'll fix him," threatened Agatha, frowning fiercely. She jumped up and ran smack into Cornelia.

"Whoa!" said Cornelia. "What's the matter, Agatha?" She looked around at the girls. "Why do you all look so sour?"

"Not sour," explained Samantha. "Salty. Eddie Ryland put salt in the ice cream and it's *ruined*."

Aunt Cornelia tasted the ice cream. "My stars!" she said. "You're right!" She looked at the disappointed girls. "Well," she said briskly, "you certainly can't eat *that*! But you still have lovely petit fours and delicious lemonade. Just ignore the ice cream."

All the girls carefully pushed the bowls of salty ice cream toward the center of the table. They ate their petit fours in silence. Samantha could hardly swallow, she felt so angry and sad. Her beautiful, elegant birthday party had been spoiled. But Agnes and Agatha finished eating quickly and hurried away from the table. They whispered with Cornelia for a few moments, then bounded back over to Samantha.

"We have the most wonderful idea!" crowed Agnes.

"You're going to come to New York!"

"Ooooh!" sighed all the girls. "New York!"

"Cornelia says if it's all right with Grandmary, you can come to New York and stay at her new house," said Agatha.

"You can come next week," said Agnes. "We'll be there, too, and we can all go to Tyson's Ice Cream Parlor for the best ice cream in New York."

"With no Eddie Ryland to spoil it," said Agatha, the fierce gleam back in her eyes.

"I'd love that," said Samantha. The twins' latest idea made the disappointment of salty ice cream melt away. "May I go?" she asked Grandmary.

"Of course you may," said Grandmary. "And I shall go with you. I've been looking forward to peppermint ice cream myself!"

New York City

ew York City! Just the name was magic! Samantha leaned forward to peek out of the horse-drawn cab. She and Grandmary were riding along the busy city streets from the train station to Gard and Cornelia's new house. Samantha held on to her hat and twisted her head around, trying to see to the tops of the buildings. Everything in New York was so big! There were so many people hurrying along the sidewalks. In New York it always seemed as if something exciting was about to happen.

"I can't wait to see Agnes and Agatha," Samantha said to Grandmary.

"You do have a good time with them, don't you, dear?" said Grandmary.

"They're always so much fun," said Samantha.

"They are happy, lively girls," agreed Grandmary.

"Though they can get carried away with their ideas."

Samantha understood what Grandmary meant about Agnes and Agatha. Sometimes their ideas were as tangled as their bouncy red curls. "They're always thinking up new ways to do things," Samantha went on.

"Yes," said Grandmary. "But I'm afraid they don't always think very carefully. Besides, they don't realize that many times the old ways are still the best ways."

Suddenly, the cab jerked to a stop. Grandmary and Samantha leaned forward to look out. They were stopped at the edge of a big park. The sidewalk was so crowded, people spilled out into the street. Samantha saw some women hanging large banners across the entrance to the park. One banner said "WOMEN, FIGHT FOR YOUR RIGHT TO VOTE." Another banner said "NOW IS THE TIME FOR CHANGE."

"We'll have to go another way, ma'am," the cab driver called down to Grandmary. "These ladies seem to be blocking traffic all around Madison Square Park."

"Very well," Grandmary answered, sitting back. She didn't seem to want to look at what was going on.

But Samantha stared out the window of the cab. She

was fascinated. "What's happening here?" she asked Grandmary.

"Well, it appears that a group of women is having a meeting in that park," Grandmary replied.

"Who are they?" Samantha asked.

"They're suffragists," Grandmary answered. "They think women should be able to vote, so they gather and make a ruckus about changing the laws." She sat up very straight. "It's all just newfangled notions."

The cab turned down a quieter street and Samantha sat back. She was still very curious about the meeting in the park, but she could tell by the look on Grandmary's face that she should not ask any more questions about it.

They rode in silence until the cab stopped in front of Gard and Cornelia's tall, narrow brownstone house. Samantha had just hopped out onto the sidewalk when she heard voices shouting, "Samantha! Samantha!" She looked up. Agnes and Agatha were leaning out of a window high above her, waving wildly. Agnes held up Jip and waved his paw. Jip barked and wriggled with joy.

"Hello!" Samantha called. She skipped and waved,

already swept away by the twins' high spirits.

"We'll be right down!" Agatha yelled. Then she and Agnes and Jip disappeared from the window.

Cornelia smiled as she came down the front steps to Samantha and Grandmary. "Welcome!" she said. Just then the twins and Jip came flying out the door and down the steps. "Hurray! You're here!" they said as they hugged Samantha. Aunt Cornelia laughed. "Come in, come in," she said. "As you can see, we're all very glad you're here."

The twins led Samantha into the dark, cool house. Uncle Gard was waiting just inside the doorway. He blinked at Samantha and said, "There you are, Sam! I've been looking for you all week long. I can't seem to find anything in this new house."

"Do you think you could help us find some lunch?" asked Aunt Cornelia.

"Certainly, certainly," said Uncle Gard, kissing the tip of her nose. "When it comes to finding food, I never have any trouble."

"Come on, Samantha!" said Agnes and Agatha. They pulled her into the dining room and made her sit between them. Then, both at once, they began showering her with questions. "Have you seen that terrible Eddie? How was your train ride? Do you want to go to the park after lunch? Do you want—"

"Girls!" Aunt Cornelia scolded gently as the maid began to pass the food. "You'll put Samantha in a spin with all your questions! There will be plenty of time for chatter later. I haven't even had a chance to ask Grandmary where she plans to shop today."

"I'll shop at O'Neill's, of course," replied Grandmary. "I never go any farther."

"There's a fine new shop on Fifth Avenue that's closer than O'Neill's," said Uncle Gard. "What was the name of that store, Cornelia?"

Grandmary patted his arm and smiled. "Don't trouble yourself to remember, Gardner," she said. "I shall go to O'Neill's. I've shopped there for more than thirty years. I'm too old to change my ways now."

"O'Neill's is near Madison Square Park," said Aunt Cornelia slowly. "That area may be quite crowded today. There's a meeting in the park."

"I know," said Grandmary. "We passed it on our way from the station. Those suffragists were already blocking traffic." She shook her head. "In my opinion, ladies should not gather in public places. *Especially* not to carry on about this voting nonsense."

"Nonsense?" Aunt Cornelia asked. Her voice rose ever so slightly.

"Of course," said Grandmary. "Voting is not a lady's concern. It never has been. I see no reason to change things now. Those suffragists are making spectacles of themselves. They should stay at home where ladies belong."

Samantha saw Agnes and Agatha look at each other with raised eyebrows, then quickly look down into their soup bowls.

Aunt Cornelia opened her mouth to say something, then shut it again.

Samantha was bursting with curiosity. "But why—?" she began to ask.

"Well, well, well," interrupted Uncle Gard. "Well, well. The strangest thing happened to me as I was walking home from work the other day. A man came up to me and said, 'Do you know any girls who just turned ten years old?' And I said, 'Why, yes, in fact I do know one.' And he said, 'Would you give her this large box? There's something inside she might like.'

So I brought the box home. It's out in the hall. Perhaps you'll open it, Sam, and show us what's inside."

Samantha forgot all about her questions. She and the twins ran from the table and opened the door. Jip was waiting right outside. He barked and jumped as the twins helped Samantha tear off the wrapping paper and open the box. Inside was a pram—the prettiest doll carriage Samantha had ever seen. It was deep red with shiny brass wheels. "Jiminy!" Samantha whispered. "It's beautiful." She ran to give Uncle Gard a big hug. "Thank you, Uncle Gard. Thank you very much!" She knew perfectly well the doll carriage was from Uncle Gard and no one else.

"Let's take it to Gramercy Park right now," suggested Agnes, who was as excited as Samantha.

"That *would* be fun." Samantha said eagerly. "May we go?"

"Certainly," said Uncle Gard.

"Can Jip come, too?" asked Agatha. "You know how he loves the park."

"No, I don't think that is a good idea," said Aunt Cornelia. "Remember what happened at Samantha's party when he ran away from you?"

"Oh, but nothing like that will happen *here*," said Agatha quickly. "The park has a fence all around it."

"Please, please, please?" begged Agnes.

Aunt Cornelia thought for a moment.

"We'll only be across the street in the park," wheedled Agatha.

"And you won't go any farther than that?" asked Aunt Cornelia.

"No!" the twins promised together.

"Will you keep Jip on his leash?"

"Yes!" shouted the girls.

"Promise?"

"Absolutely!" they cried.

"Well, all right," Cornelia finally agreed. "But—"

"Hurray!" the twins interrupted. Jip began yipping in excitement.

"Please be calm for just a minute," Aunt Cornelia said seriously. "I'm going to a meeting, but I'll be back at three-thirty. When I get back, we'll walk to the ice cream parlor to meet Grandmary. Don't forget."

"And don't forget to behave like young ladies," added Grandmary.

"And don't forget the rule about keeping Jip on the

leash," repeated Aunt Cornelia.

"And don't forget to have a good time," said Uncle Gard, shaking his finger at them.

"We won't!" said the girls. And Jip barked to show that he agreed.

Follow That Dog!

ip led a very cheerful parade to Gramercy Park. He pranced along the sidewalk, pulling at his leash. Agnes and Agatha skipped to keep up with him. Samantha followed behind, proudly pushing her new doll carriage. Even the doll Agnes had loaned her, which was rather tired looking, seemed to perk up as she rode in the fine red pram out in the midday sunshine.

Gramercy Park was a pretty rectangular green across the street from Gard and Cornelia's house. It was fenced on all four sides by tall black iron railings with two locked gates. The buildings that surrounded it seemed to look down on the quiet little park fondly, as if they wanted to protect it from the hubbub of the city.

Agnes unlocked one gate, and the girls followed Jip into the park. He zigzagged from one side of the path to the other, sniffing out interesting scents as he led the girls to a large fountain in the center of the park. Around the bottom of the fountain there was a pool where tin swans swam. "How pretty," said Samantha. "The swans look almost real."

Jip seemed to agree with Samantha. He growled at the swans and dragged on his leash, trying to get at them.

"Stop it, Jip," scolded Agatha, jerking him back. She tried to pull Jip away, but he lunged and leaped, barking wildly all the while. "Jip's pulling my arm out," complained Agatha.

"You'd better carry him," suggested Samantha.

So Agatha picked Jip up, but he kept barking even when they walked away from the fountain. When Agatha put him down, Jip tried to run back to the swans, so she had to pick him up again. He squirmed in her arms. "I'm tired of carrying Jip," Agatha whined. "You take him, Agnes."

"Absolutely not," said Agnes. "He'll get paw prints all over my dress. I don't want to be a mess like you are. After all," she said in a hoity-toity voice, "ladies do not make spectacles of themselves."

Samantha had to laugh. Agnes sounded just like Grandmary.

"Well, it's not fair," grumbled Agatha. "I've carried Jip enough. It was your dumb idea to bring him."

"It was not," said Agnes.

"It was too," said Agatha.

"It was not."

"It was too."

"Oh, *I'll* carry him," Samantha said firmly. "You push the pram, Agatha."

Agatha eyed the doll carriage. "No," she said. "I have a better idea."

"What now?" asked Agnes.

"Let's put Jip in the pram. That way none of us will have to carry him," said Agatha.

Agnes was instantly enthusiastic. "Oh, that *is* a good idea!" she said. "He can sit right next to the doll."

But Samantha didn't think it sounded like such a good idea. "We promised Cornelia we wouldn't let Jip off the leash," she reminded the twins.

"We're not going to let *Jip* off the leash," said Agatha. "We're going to let *me* off the leash. Just watch." Agatha slipped the leash off her wrist and put

Jip in the pram. She looped the leash over the handle of the pram. "There! You see?" she said. "He's perfectly safe."

Samantha shook her head. "I don't think—"

Agnes interrupted, "Oh, don't be such a worrywart, Samantha. This is a brand-new way to walk a dog. It's a great idea. Doesn't Jip look cute?"

And Jip did look cute, but only for one second. He yanked the leash with his mouth and pulled it off the handle. Then, before the girls could grab him, he leaped out of the carriage and took off like a streak.

"STOP!" shouted Samantha. "Jip, stop!" She started to run after him, trying to grab the leash dragging in the dirt.

"Jip! Jip! Jip! Jip! Jip!" Agatha yelped. She hopped up and down, waving her arms.

"Oh, no!" wailed all three girls when they saw Jip wiggle between the iron bars of the fence and slip out of the park. Just for a second, he turned to look at them.

"What'll we do now?" groaned Agnes. "Cornelia will be furious!"

"Quick! Climb over the fence!" yelled Agatha wildly. She ran to the fence and started to shinny up the iron bars. "Split up! Get the firemen! Call the police!"

Agnes just stood still, holding her face in her hands, moaning.

Samantha saw that she was going to have to take charge. "Don't just stand there," she ordered. "We've got to catch him. Come on!" She led the twins to the gate and pushed it open. They could see Jip halfway down the block, his white tail waving like a feather as he trotted along. The gate swung shut behind them.

"Your doll carriage!" cried Agnes.

"Leave it," Samantha said as she ran. "We've got to get Jip."

The three girls took off after Jip. He was running toward a big hotel on the corner. Samantha saw a group of people waiting in front with piles of luggage around them. "Stop that dog!" she called. But Jip was too fast. He bounded through the crowd, jumped over a trunk, and slipped around the corner.

As the girls dashed after him, Samantha heard a frightening rumble. A shower of soot fell like black snow. She looked up for one second to see a train running along a track built up over the street. When she looked down again, Jip had disappeared.

"Where'd he go?" she gasped to Agnes.

"I don't know," Agnes wailed. "We've lost him. Forever and ever!"

"Not if I can help it!" said Samantha. She ran up to a man pushing a cart full of strawberries. "Have you seen our dog?" she asked urgently.

"Yes, yes!" said the man. "He went that way." He pointed farther up the street.

"Thanks!" yelled Samantha.

"There he is!" shouted Agatha. They saw Jip's tail bouncing along ahead of a wagon overflowing with flowers. The wagon looked just like Grandmary's garden in Mount Bedford. But chasing Jip in New York City was a lot different from chasing him in Mount Bedford. The city was so big, and Jip was so little. What if they lost him? What if—

Clang! Clang! Clang!

Samantha practically jumped out of her skin as a big streetcar rumbled up to the curb in front of her. The huge, sweaty horses that pulled it shook their harnesses, snorting as they waited for people to get off. Samantha looked at the heavy hooves and thought how easily Jip could be crushed by them.

"Now where is he?" cried Agnes.

"I see him," said Agatha. "On the other side of the street."

The girls dashed across the street, weaving between a wagon full of rattling milk cans and an automobile whose horn blared at them. Jip was far ahead of them now, slithering like a snake through the crowd. It was hard for the girls to move very fast because the sidewalk was so full of people. The girls had to wiggle their way between fashionable ladies, gentlemen in straw hats, boys selling newspapers, and workmen carrying heavy loads. "'Scuse me, 'scuse me," said Samantha as she and the twins jostled past the people.

Agatha tripped over a loose brick in the sidewalk and fell to her knees. "Ow!" she wailed, almost in tears. "Go ahead, leave me behind."

"No," said Samantha. She helped Agatha get up and dusted her off. "You're fine. Come on," she said. "You can't stop now. We need you. You're the best one at spotting Jip."

None of them saw Jip again until they got to the corner of Fifth Avenue, the widest and busiest street in

New York. "Look!" called Agatha, pointing with both hands. "There's Jip! In the street!"

Samantha leaped off the curb to get him when suddenly the pavement shook beneath her feet. Someone yanked her back up onto the sidewalk. She was almost crushed in the tumble of people who scrambled to get back on the curb. "Watch out!" a voice shouted. "Fire engine! Out of the way!"

"JIP!" yelled Samantha. She caught a glimpse of Jip, but then two huge horses galloped in front of her, pulling a fire engine. Its deafening bell rang out over the shouts and screams from the crowd. The firemen clung to the shiny pump in the middle of the wagon as it stormed past in a blur of red and silver, stirring up a cloud of dust in the street, racing like the wind.

"Jip," Samantha whispered. Was Jip somewhere in that cloud of dust? Nothing moved in the street. "Oh, Jip, we never should have let you go."

Changes

The fire engine roared off around the corner. The dust settled. Samantha stood on the curb, gathering her courage to go out into the street and look for Jip.

Agnes and Agatha ran up to her. "Where is he?" Agnes asked breathlessly. "Where's Jip? Do you see him?"

Samantha shook her head no. "I think he might . . . he might be . . ."

"There he is!" shouted Agatha, hopping up and down. "Look! He's going into that park across the street."

"I see him!" shouted Samantha. She was so relieved. "Come on! Now we've *got* to catch him."

The girls dashed across the street into the park. Jip trip-trotted ahead of them as if he knew exactly

where he was going and nothing would stop him.
He darted through a crowd of women who were all
headed toward a platform draped with signs and flags.

"Oh, no," Agnes gulped. "This is Madison Square
Park, where the suffragists' meeting is!"

"Quick, let's get out of here!" said Agatha in a panic.

"No," said Samantha. "We've got to get Jip. Grandmary won't mind if we're in the park for just a minute
to get the dog."

"It's not Grandmary we're worried about,"
interrupted Agnes. "It's Cornelia. She's here. And if
she sees us, she'll be furious. She thinks we're back in
Gramercy Park."

"Cornelia?" Samantha gasped. "What's *she* doing
here?"

"She's at the meeting about women voting," Agatha
said quickly. "We heard her tell Gard she was coming.
He said Grandmary wouldn't like it. But Cornelia
said she could think for herself and she was coming
anyway."

Samantha was very confused. What was Cornelia
doing with the suffragists? Grandmary said these
women were making spectacles of themselves. Was

Cornelia doing something wrong? But Samantha didn't have time to think. Agnes grabbed her arm. "Come on!" she ordered. "Let's get Jip and *go*."

The girls chased Jip to a small pool with a fountain in the middle. He eyed the girls. As they came closer, he edged away. "Give him some room," said Samantha. "We don't want him to—"

Splash! Jip jumped into the pool!

"I'll dive in and get him!" Agatha cried. She pulled off her shoe.

"WAIT!" said Samantha quickly. She grabbed Agatha's shoe and waved it in front of Jip, just as she had in Mount Bedford. "Look, Jip," she said in a friendly voice. "A shoe. Come and get it."

Jip looked at the shoe. He began to paddle across the pool toward Samantha. Just then, the crowd got very quiet. "Ladies and gentlemen," a woman's voice began.

Jip stopped. He tilted his head and perked up his ears. When the speaker said "Welcome," Jip yelped with joy. He sprang out of the pool, splattering water all over the girls. Before they could grab him, he scampered up the steps of the speakers' platform, yipping and yapping wildly. He ran right up to the woman who was standing in front of everyone.

"CORNELIA!" gasped all three girls. The speaker was Cornelia! Jip wiggled from head to tail, sending a spray of water all over her.

"Jip? What are you doing here?" Cornelia asked. Jip barked excitedly, and she scooped him up in her arms. "Well," she said, turning to the crowd, "this eager fellow wants to speak, too!"

The crowd clapped and laughed.

Cornelia's voice was strong and firm as she went on. "The time has come for all of us to speak out. We must stand up for what we believe is right!" she said. "We must make up our own minds. The time has come to change the old ways. Women *must* vote!"

The crowd clapped louder than ever. Some women waved banners and cheered. Cornelia carried Jip back to her seat, and another woman rose to speak. As Cornelia sat down, she looked all around, searching for faces in the crowd.

"Jeepers! She's looking for us!" whispered Agnes.

"Well, she's got Jip, so let's get out of here!" said Agatha.

"No," said Samantha. "We can't do that. We have to face her and admit what we did."

The twins looked at each other uncomfortably.

"Maybe you're right," sighed Agatha.

The girls waited nervously while other suffragists spoke. When all the speeches were over and the crowd had begun to wander away, Cornelia came down from the platform. She walked toward the girls. "Well," she said without a trace of her usual smile. "What are *you*—and Jip—doing here?"

The girls looked down at their shoes. "We did a very stupid thing," Samantha began.

"It was really a terrible idea," admitted Agnes.

"We put Jip in the pram," said Samantha. "And we didn't hold on to the leash, so he ran away."

Agatha burst out, "But we didn't think that he'd—"

"You certainly *didn't* think," Cornelia cut in. "You just went right ahead with your own ideas and didn't pay any attention to what I said about keeping Jip on the leash. That was an important rule and one we all agreed on. When will you girls learn that you can't just change things when you feel like it?"

"But aren't you trying to change things?" asked

Agatha. "Aren't you trying to get women to vote?"

"That's very different, Agatha," answered Cornelia. "All the women here today have thought long and hard about changing the laws so that women can vote. When you want to change something, you'd better be sure it's a wise change, a change for the better."

The girls were silent. Finally Samantha said, "We're very sorry, Aunt Cornelia. We really are."

Cornelia shook her head. "I believe you are sorry," she said. "You certainly look sorry. In fact, you look like a sorry mess." Her voice had a little laugh in it. She looked at her watch. "Oh, my gracious! It's nearly three-thirty. We'll be late meeting Grandmary if we don't leave right now. There's no time to go home and change. We'll have to go to Tyson's as untidy as we are."

The girls were rumpled and wrinkled, and Cornelia's dress was covered with muddy paw prints, so it was a very bedraggled parade that Jip led to the ice cream parlor. When they got to Tyson's, Samantha saw Grandmary sitting at a corner table near the gleaming soda fountain. Her face was rather red, and Samantha was afraid she might be angry.

Samantha rushed ahead of Cornelia and the twins. "Grandmary," she blurted out, "we're sorry to be so late and sorry that we look so messy, but we've had the most awful time. Agnes and Agatha and I nearly lost Jip. We chased him everywhere, and finally he ran into Madison Square Park. Remember, the place where the cab stopped this morning? Jip jumped into a fountain there, and just when we almost caught him, he got away again. But it was all right because he ran onto the speakers' platform and right up to—" Samantha stopped. "Oh, no," she said. She didn't want to tell Grandmary about Cornelia.

But Cornelia finished for Samantha. "Jip ran right up to *me*," she said, looking Grandmary straight in the eye. "*I* was on the speakers' platform."

"I know you were on the platform," said Grandmary. "I saw you. I was at the meeting myself."

"You were?" everyone gasped.

"Yes," said Grandmary firmly. "I was on my way here to Tyson's. But there were so many people around the park that I couldn't get by. When I saw *you* up on the platform, Cornelia, I thought perhaps I ought to stay and listen." Grandmary took Cornelia's hand.

"My dear," she said, "I must admit that what I saw and what I heard gave me a bit of a surprise. I've said that I'm too old to change my ways, but I've changed my mind today."

Samantha saw that Grandmary's hat was tipped back a little, as if she'd turned around very suddenly. "You and the other ladies who spoke today were simply saying that women should stand up for what they think is right. That's exactly what I believe, too. And if that's what voting will give us a chance to do, then I think women *should* vote. The time for change *has* come."

Cornelia smiled at Grandmary. "Yes, it is time to change the old rules," she said. "And that's what makes this a wonderful time for these young ladies to be growing up."

"Well, growing up is what we've come to celebrate," said Grandmary. "Shall we have our ice cream?"

She turned to Samantha. "Peppermint for you, my dear? Or would you like to try something new today?"

"No, thank you," smiled Samantha. "Peppermint is my old favorite. There are some things that are just too good to change."

Piney Point

CHAPTER 6

everal weeks later, Samantha stood at the end of the dock at the edge of Goose Lake. *Too-oot!* With a cheerful blast of its whistle, a little steamboat chugged across the lake toward Samantha. Its snappy red and white awning flapped in the breeze. Samantha skipped on her tiptoes, waving both arms wildly to welcome the boat and its passengers.

"Yoo-hoo! Hello!" she called. "Agnes! Agatha! Hello!" As the boat came closer, Samantha could see Agnes and Agatha standing on the deck, waving hello to her. Their red curls were as bright as poppies in the sunshine. The twins were coming to stay at Piney Point, Grandmary's summer home in the mountains. Uncle Gard and Aunt Cornelia were with them. And so was Admiral Archibald Beemis. He came all the

47

way from England every summer to visit Grandmary. Samantha danced with excitement. It was wonderful to have all of her favorite people together at her favorite place in the world. They would be just like a big happy family!

The boat pulled up to the dock, and Agnes and Agatha jumped ashore.

"Samantha!" they cried together. "Hello!" They swooped up to hug her. "We're finally here!"

"Agatha was seasick," announced Agnes.

"I was *not*," protested Agatha.

"She was too," Agnes went on. "And we weren't even on the boat yet. We were on the sleeper train from Albany and—"

"Girls!" laughed Aunt Cornelia as she kissed Samantha hello. "Tell Samantha later. Right now you'd better scoot out of the way of the luggage."

The girls stepped back as the boatmen unloaded satchels and trunks, wicker baskets, and suitcases onto the dock. Uncle Gard and Admiral Beemis appeared behind the enormous pile of luggage. Uncle Gard was trying to carry two hatboxes, a parasol, and a picnic hamper. "Pardon me, miss," he said to Samantha.

"Did I get off at the wrong stop? Is this Grand Central Station, New York?"

"No!" giggled Samantha. "It's Piney Point, Uncle Gard. Finally, finally everyone's here at Piney Point."

"Right-oh!" boomed the Admiral. He beamed with delight and saluted Samantha. His twinkly eyes were as blue as the lake.

Samantha saluted back. "Welcome ashore, Admiral," she said. "Grandmary will be so happy to see you. We've both been waiting all morning."

Samantha led everyone up the steep hillside to the house. The twins exclaimed happily each step of the way.

"It's so cool here!"

"It smells like Christmas trees!"

"Oooh! Look! A log cabin! It's huge!"

Grandmary was standing on the shady porch of the big log house. She looked as cool and serene as a cloud in her white summer dress.

"Welcome to Piney Point, my dears," she said to the twins. "Gardner, Cornelia, hello!" She smiled as she held out her hand to the Admiral. "Archie! How lovely to see you!"

"Lovely indeed!" repeated the Admiral. "Mary, you look as lovely as the day I met you, more than thirty years ago." He bowed over her hand and kissed it.

Grandmary laughed, a little pink in the cheeks. "Oh, Archie, I am glad you're here. It doesn't seem like summer until you arrive."

"Summer it is," said Uncle Gard. "And I feel as boiled as a summer squash after that trip. Who's for a swim?"

"Me!" cried all the girls together.

"All right," said Uncle Gard. He was already loosening his tie. "I'll meet you at the lake in five minutes. Last one in is a rotten egg."

"Come on," Samantha said to the twins. "Let's go and change."

"Wait," said Agnes as she followed Samantha down the porch steps. "Where are we going? We don't have to live out in the woods, do we?"

Samantha grinned. "No. One of the best things about Piney Point is that we all have our own little houses. The Admiral stays over the boathouse. Uncle Gard and Aunt Cornelia are in the Rose Cottage. And *this* is ours." She flung open the door to a one-room cottage. It had three tall windows facing the lake. Samantha had filled big baskets with goldenrod and black-eyed Susans. Their fresh, woodsy scent filled the little house.

"Is this house for the three of us?" asked Agatha. "Just us and no grownups?"

"That's right," said Samantha. "Just us."

"I absolutely love it!" sighed Agnes. She flopped onto one of the three beds and looked around. "Look at that chair made out of tree branches. The branches are so shiny and twisted together, the chair looks like it's made out of pretzels."

"Our little house is like a treehouse," said Agatha as she leaned out a window into the waving branches of a pine tree. "Does it have a name, too?"

"Mmm hmm," answered Samantha. She was pulling her bathing suit over her head. "It's called Wood Tick Inn."

"Wood *Tick*?" asked Agnes uncertainly. She sat up suddenly and looked into the corners of the room. "Ticks are bugs, aren't they? Is it called Wood Tick Inn because it's full of horrible bugs?"

"No!" laughed Samantha. "Not horrible bugs. But

you *might* see a few ladybugs or spiders—"

"Spiders?" Agnes clutched her bathing suit to her chest.

"Oh, honestly, Agnes," said Agatha as she pulled off her long stockings. "You're not in the city now. This is the wilderness. There's *supposed* to be wildlife here. We'll probably see lots of bears and wolves and hear coyotes howling in the night. Isn't that right, Samantha?"

"Well, I've never seen any bears or wolves," said Samantha. "But there are lots of other animals to see, like deer and moose and rabbits. And the lake is full of fish."

"Do the fish bite?" asked Agnes.

"Of course not!" said Samantha. "Unless your toes look like worms! Come on, let's go swimming." She led the twins down a path covered with pine needles to the edge of the water.

"Look," said Agatha. "Gard and the Admiral are out on that big rock in the lake. Let's swim to them."

"All right," agreed Samantha.

"I think I'll just wade," said Agnes. She timidly put one toe in the water.

"I don't know what's the matter with her," said Agatha as she and Samantha splashed into the lake. "She's brave enough in the city, but here she acts like a scaredy-cat about little things like bugs and fish. Really!"

"Don't worry," said Samantha. "She'll get over it. Nobody stays fussy or scared at Piney Point. Come on! I'll race you to the rock."

And Samantha was absolutely right. Piney Point quickly worked its magic on Agnes. In just a few days, she was splashing straight into the lake, right along with the other girls. When the Admiral took them trout fishing, Agnes even put the worms on the hook with her own fingers.

Every day at Piney Point was filled with something wonderful to discover. In the morning Mrs. Hawkins gave the girls sandwiches to put in their pack baskets, and off they went exploring. Samantha showed Agnes and Agatha where sweet red raspberries grew on the hillside. She led them to a sunny meadow where they caught butterflies with their long-handled nets.

The three girls canoed to the marsh. There turtles sunned themselves on the rocks, noisy birds nested in the cattails, and frogs poked just their eyes out of the water. One day they saw a mother deer and her fawn very near their house, and once they watched a big elk drinking out of the lake.

From early morning, when the gauzy mist rose off the lake, until late at night when lightning bugs twinkled all around them like falling stars, the girls were so happy and busy that the long summer days just flew past. After two weeks at Piney Point, the twins' noses were sprinkled with freckles and their hair was golden orange. So the Admiral called them "the Tiger Lilies."

The Admiral was one of the best parts of Piney Point. Each afternoon he joined Samantha, Agnes, and Agatha for a swim. He paddled along with his head raised out of the water, like a duck. Sometimes he invited the girls along when he took Grandmary out rowing in the moonlight. He gave Samantha a genuine bo's'n's whistle made of shiny brass and taught her how to blow signals like the sailors did. And he gave all three girls sailor hats, which they proudly wore whenever they went boating on the lake.

One hot, still day, the girls were picking wild-flowers on the rocky hill behind the main house. Samantha raced ahead of the twins and scrambled up to the top of a big boulder. She held an imaginary spyglass up to one eye and looked all around her. "Who am I?" she asked Agatha.

"You're Admiral Archibald Beemis!" Agatha cried. She climbed up on the boulder next to Samantha.

"Right-oh!" Samantha replied with a salute.

"Gosh," panted Agnes as she climbed up on the rock, too. "You can see all over from up here. You can really see why they call it Goose Lake. Over there is the goose's thin neck, and there's its head. That big island is its eye."

"Look at that pretty little island just below the goose's eye," said Agatha. "What's that called, Samantha?"

"That's Teardrop Island," Samantha answered. She climbed down from the boulder.

"Oh, because it's shaped like a teardrop," Agnes said.

"Do you see that rocky cliff?" asked Agatha. She

pointed to a cliff at the end of Teardrop Island. "I'd love to climb that. I bet you can see all the way to New York from there."

"I have a great idea," exclaimed Agnes. "Let's go to Teardrop Island tomorrow. We can go in the canoe and take a picnic and stay all day!"

"That would be fun," agreed Agatha. "We could bring our paints, too."

"No," said Samantha.

But the twins didn't hear her. "We can be real explorers," Agatha went on. "We can hike from one end of the island to the other."

"No," Samantha said again, louder. "I don't want to go there."

The twins were surprised. "Why not?"

"Because it's . . . it's not a good place," said Samantha. She pushed her sweaty bangs off her forehead.

"But it looks so pretty," said Agatha. "What's the matter with it?"

"Are there bears and wolves on the island?" asked Agnes. "Is it dangerous?"

"The island isn't dangerous, but you have to go

through that narrow part of the lake to get there," said Samantha. "It's filled with big sharp rocks."

"We can steer around those rocks," said Agatha. "That's easy!"

"The dangerous rocks are hidden underwater. You can't see them, but they can still rip out the bottom of your boat," said Samantha. She was quiet for a moment. Then she said softly, "That's where my mother and father drowned. There was a storm, and their boat was wrecked on the rocks. They were on their way back from Teardrop Island."

"Oh!" said both twins. They looked very sad.

"That's terrible, Samantha," said Agatha quietly. "That's just terrible."

"We're awfully sorry," said Agnes. "We didn't know about . . . about what happened there. We didn't mean to make you feel bad, Samantha, really we didn't."

"I know," said Samantha. She bent down to pick some wildflowers growing near the boulder. "It's just that I hate to even think about Teardrop Island. It makes me sad, and scared, too. I never want to go there. Not *ever*."

"I don't want to go there either," said Agatha.

"Me either," said Agnes. "Besides, there are plenty of other places we can go and things we can do."

"That's right," agreed Agatha. "There are millions of things to do at Piney Point. Let's go swimming. It's too hot to pick any more flowers."

"We'll race you, Samantha." said Agnes. "Come on."

The three girls ran very fast down the hill toward the shining blue lake.

That night it was still very hot. The Admiral helped the girls drag their mattresses out to the little porch on Wood Tick Inn so they could sleep out in the soft, warm breeze from the lake. There was a patch of velvety black sky above them, framed by the tops of pine trees. Hundreds of stars glittered and winked at them.

The girls stretched out on their backs with their heads together. "There are lots more stars here than there are in the city," said Agnes.

"And they're much closer," said Agatha.

"Mmm," agreed Samantha.

The girls could hear waves lapping peacefully against the shore. The murmur of the adults' voices

drifted up from the porch of the main house where
Grandmary, Uncle Gard, Aunt Cornelia, and the
Admiral sat to catch the breeze. Once in a while, the
murmur turned into laughter. The girls could hear the
Admiral's loud, hearty "Haw! Haw!"

Samantha smiled. "I love the way the Admiral
laughs. He sounds like a happy donkey."

"He's the best grownup I've ever met," stated
Agnes. "He's not afraid of anything. He's not bossy.
And he knows interesting things. He knows more
about this place than anyone."

"He's been coming here a long time," said
Samantha. "He was my grandfather's best friend.
After Grandpa died, he kept coming anyway, all the
way from England, every summer." She rolled over
onto her stomach. "Can you keep a secret?" she
whispered.

"Yes!" exclaimed the twins. They rolled over onto
their stomachs, too, and wiggled up close to Samantha.

Samantha kept her voice at a whisper. "I heard
Mrs. Hawkins tell Elsa once that every summer the
Admiral asks Grandmary to marry him."

"Gosh," breathed the twins.

"I guess Grandmary always says no," sighed Agatha. "I wonder why."

"Doesn't she like him?" asked Agnes.

"I don't know," said Samantha. "I think she likes him a lot."

"Well," said Agnes definitely, "if they ever did get married, you'd have a great grandfather."

"You mean a step-grandfather," corrected Agatha.

"I mean a grandfather who is great," said Agnes. "I think the Admiral would be the best grandfather in the world."

"So do I," said Samantha. She put her cheek down on her hands and closed her eyes. The soft breeze soon sang her to sleep.

The Sketchbook

A dreary gray sky hung over the girls the next morning. During breakfast, it started to rain. The rain fell hard and heavy, swooping in sheets across the lake, ribboning down the windowpanes. By midmorning the ground looked like soupy chocolate pudding.

Agnes moaned, "How can it rain so hard? The sky was perfectly clear last night."

"The weather can change very quickly here on these mountain lakes," said the Admiral. "Sunny one minute, rainy the next." He peered out the window. "We're in for it today. This is a real summer storm. Time to batten down the hatches! Foul weather ahead!"

The three girls just looked at him with faces as mopey as the moose over the mantel. "It's only eleven o'clock in the morning and we've already done

absolutely everything there is to do," complained
Samantha. It was true. They had helped Mrs. Hawkins
make bread. They had been shooed out of Wood
Tick Inn by a maid who wanted to dust. They had
watched the boatman fix the big red canoe in the
boathouse. They had pressed every wildflower they'd
gathered the day before. Agatha had finished embroi-
dering the tiny pillow she'd stuffed with pine needles
from the evergreen trees. Samantha had rearranged
all the postcards in her album. Agnes had worked on
jigsaw puzzles for hours. The three girls had run out of
indoor things to do.

"Well," said the Admiral cheerily, "since we can't go
fishing we might as well play Old Maid, eh what?"

And so until lunchtime, the girls and the Admiral
played game after game of Old Maid. The Admiral
lost every game, mostly because he was so nice. "I say,
Samantha," he'd exclaim. "I've just picked up the Old
Maid." So everyone always knew when he had it in his
hand.

After lunch the grownups all took naps. "How
can they be tired when they haven't done anything all
day?" Agatha wondered out loud. She plunked herself

down on the bearskin rug in front of the fire.

"I'm bored," complained Agnes. "I wish we could go outside."

"I have an idea!" said Samantha. "Let's set up our easels and paint on the porch. That way we can be outdoors and not get wet."

"Good idea," said Agatha. "I'm going to paint a picture of you, Samantha."

It was a little windy on the porch and rather damp, but it felt good to get out of the house. The three artists got out their wooden boxes filled with tubes of paint and worked happily and quietly for a while.

Then Agatha looked over at Agnes's easel. "Jeepers, Agnes," she said. "That's an awfully big rabbit you're painting."

"It's not a rabbit," said Agnes. "It's a sailboat."

"Oh," said Agatha. "How come it has ears?"

"Those aren't ears," said Agnes crossly. "That's supposed to be a flag." She sighed. "I have a little trouble making the paint go where I want it to go."

"I know what you mean," said Samantha. "This house I'm painting looks as if a giant had stepped on it and squooshed it."

The girls giggled.

"Maybe there's something wrong with these paintbrushes," said Agatha. She looked at the bristles of her brush. "Maybe they're worn out."

"Grandmary told me there are more brushes in the attic," said Samantha. "Let's go look for them."

Samantha led the way up the wide stairs to the second floor. They tiptoed past Grandmary's door so they wouldn't disturb her nap, and climbed up the narrow stairs to the attic.

The attic was long and dark. It smelled of dried flowers and dust.

"It's spooky up here," whispered Agnes. And it was, just a little. In the corners there were old chairs covered with sheets, so they looked like lumpy ghosts. Outside, the wind swished through the treetops. The rain had calmed down to a steady, soaking shower. It sounded unhurried, as if it would stay forever. The light from the windows was so murky, the girls couldn't tell what time of day it was, or even what season.

"Oooh, look!" cried Agatha. "Hats—boxes and boxes of them!" The girls threw off the dusty lids and lifted the hats out of tissue paper. The hats were old-fashioned and frilly. They had big floppy brims and wide satin ribbons. Agnes found one with a whole bird on top, and Samantha found one with an enormous pink bow. They put the hats on and paraded in front of a greenish mirror that sent back a wavery image.

They found gloves in another box, and beads, handbags, and shoes. In one box they found a stiff corset. Beneath a pile of old riding boots, Samantha found a box of photo albums and scrapbooks. The leather books were shut fast with brass clasps. Their gold-edged pages looked as if no one had turned them in a long, long time.

Samantha sat on the floor and opened one of the heavy books. The pictures were brown and yellow and a little faded. Everyone looked very stiff and solemn.

"What is that?" asked Agatha. She sat down next to Samantha.

"It's one of Grandmary's old photograph albums," answered Samantha. "Jiminy! Here's a picture of Uncle Gard when he was little. Look at his long curls!"

"He's as roly-poly as a teddy bear," laughed Agatha.

"There he is with a fish he caught. That was taken

right here, on the dock at Piney Point," said Agnes. She was looking over Samantha's shoulder. "The fish is as big as he is!"

The girls fell into fits of giggles and sneezes from the dust.

"Is that you, Samantha?" asked Agnes, pointing to a dark-haired girl in one of the old pictures.

"No," said Samantha. "That must be my mother when she was a girl. See, it's labeled 'Lydia.'" She stared hard at the face that smiled at her from the picture.

"She looks just like you," said Agatha. "Her smile is the same as yours."

"Do you miss her and your father just awfully?" asked Agnes.

"I miss them, but I don't really remember them very much," said Samantha. "They died when I was only five." She sighed. "I wish I *could* remember more about them and the things we did together, but I really can't."

Agatha turned to the last photograph in the book. "Here's your mother again, with Grandmary. And that man must be your grandfather. Look at Uncle Gard, pretending to steer the boat!"

All three girls smiled at silly Uncle Gard. "These

pictures are funny," said Agnes. "I wonder why Grandmary keeps them hidden away up here."

"Maybe they make her sad," said Samantha. "Maybe they make her miss my mother and grandpa too much." She put the big book back in the box and pulled out a smaller maroon one. On the cover, it said "My Sketchbook." Inside, on the first page, someone had written "Happy Memories of Teardrop Island" and, below that, "Sketches and Watercolors by Lydia."

"What's this book?" asked Agatha. Her curls brushed Samantha's cheek as she leaned forward to look.

Samantha turned the pages slowly. "It looks like something my mother made," she said. "It's sketches and watercolors of Teardrop Island."

"She was a really good artist," said Agnes.

The girls were quiet as they looked through the book. There were tiny, perfect drawings of birds and squirrels, trees and butterflies. There were larger watercolor paintings, too. The colors were soft and shimmery, as if they came through the mist of a rainbow.

Near the middle of the book there was a picture that showed a little bare-legged girl standing in a shallow pool of water. She was holding on to a man's hands and smiling. Behind them was a tangle of wild roses and a beautiful waterfall tumbling down over mossy rocks. The sunlight poured through the trees, and its greenish light made the scene look like a fairyland. At the bottom of the picture it said, "Samantha at the waterfall, 1897."

"Oh, that's you!" breathed Agnes. "With your father!"

"Look at the waterfall," said Agatha. "Was it really that beautiful?"

"I don't know," said Samantha. She shook her head. "I don't remember anything about it. I didn't even know I'd ever been to Teardrop Island."

"But look," said Agnes. "The whole rest of the book is filled with pictures of you and your parents on Teardrop Island. You're having picnics and picking flowers . . ." She flipped through the pages. "It seems like it was your favorite place. It looks like your parents took you there lots of times."

Samantha stared and stared at the drawings. She had always thought Teardrop Island was a dark, sad place. But in her mother's drawings it was lovely and full of light. Teardrop Island didn't look like a place to be afraid of or a place to hate at all. Samantha turned back to the painting of the waterfall. She could almost smell the roses and feel the slippery, mossy stones under her feet. *My parents and I were together there,* she thought. *And we looked so happy!*

Suddenly she said, "Let's go there. Let's go to Teardrop Island."

Agnes and Agatha looked up at her. "But I thought you didn't want to go there, *ever,*" said Agatha.

"Well, I didn't know it was so beautiful," said Samantha. "And I didn't know I used to go there with my mother and father. I forgot. Maybe if I go back, I'll remember. I'll remember what it was like . . . and what my parents were like . . . and being together . . ." She smoothed the page under her hand. "I just have to go there. Do you want to come with me?"

"Of course!" said both twins.

"We'll go tomorrow," said Samantha. "So we'll have all day. We'd better not tell anyone."

"All right," said Agnes.

"Look!" said Agatha. "It's stopped raining. Let's go out and splash in the puddles."

Samantha followed the twins out of the shadowy attic, down the stairs, and into the bright, warm sunshine. She carried the sketchbook carefully in both hands. Now that she had found it, she never wanted to let it go.

Teardrop Island

Samantha and the twins set out early the next day. Their pack baskets were jammed with sandwiches and cookies, butterfly nets, bird guides, and magnifying glasses—the same equipment they started out with every morning. But this morning, Samantha had her mother's sketchbook tucked away under the picnic blanket in her pack basket.

The Admiral came down to the dock to help the girls push off. "Where are you off to today, mateys?" he asked.

"Just exploring," answered Agnes lightly.

"Well, keep an eye on the weather," warned the Admiral. "It could turn nasty. That storm could twist around and hit us again today. Anchors aweigh! Cheerio!"

"Cheerio!" the girls called back as their canoe glided into the deeper water. It was another hot day. The sun burned so strong, it seemed to have bleached the sky white. "As soon as we get to the island, I'm going straight to the waterfall," announced Agnes. "It looks so cool in the pictures."

"I'm climbing right up to that rocky cliff at the end of the island," said Agatha. "I can't wait to see the view."

"I want to see *everything*," said Samantha. She wondered what Teardrop Island would be like. Would it be just the way it was in her mother's pictures? Would she remember being there with her parents? Would it seem friendly and familiar, or scary and strange?

The lake was flat and peaceful. The girls paddled steadily, and soon Piney Point was out of sight.

"Watch it! Rocks ahead!" warned Agatha from the front of the canoe. The lake was suddenly narrow. Steep hills rose up on either side. Big boulders stuck up out of the water. Jagged rocks hid just below the surface. The water churned white where it splashed against the rocks.

The girls were quiet. They gripped their paddles and steered carefully. They had to zig and zag to find the best path around the sharp rocks.

"Go to the left!" Agatha would shout, and then, "Quick! To the right!" Samantha felt sweat from heat and fear dripping down her back. But the canoe was high in the water, so it slipped smoothly over the rocks beneath it. And it was so slender, it slithered between the boulders as easily as a fish.

Finally, they were through the narrow passage and into a wider, deeper part of the lake.

"Phew!" said Samantha.

"We did it!" cheered Agatha, waving her paddle over her head.

"I bet even the Admiral couldn't have done better," boasted Agnes.

Now the canoe seemed to float by itself across the water into the cool shadow of Teardrop Island. As they came near the island, the girls could hear a chorus of birds singing gaily, as if the island itself were welcoming them. They saw a small stretch of pebbly shore where they could land the canoe. The rest of the shore was made up of big rocks.

As soon as the water was shallow enough, Agatha hopped out of the canoe and pulled the front end out of the water and up onto the pebbly shore. Samantha and Agnes quickly gathered up their pack baskets and climbed out, too. They were so excited, they rushed up the steep shore and into the piney woods.

"We're here!" crowed Agnes. They threaded their way between the tall pine trees and moss-covered rocks. There seemed to be an old path, but it was so overgrown with giant ferns and long grass, it was hard to tell. Overhead, leaves fluttered hello and squirrels leaped from tree to tree, inspecting their visitors.

"It's like a jungle!" exclaimed Agatha as she batted a branch away. "Now we're really explorers."

"It looks like the enchanted forest in *Sleeping Beauty*," said Samantha. "It's as if it's been under a spell for a hundred years, just waiting for us to come."

The branches of the trees hung so low over the path, it was like walking through a green tunnel. But once in a while, the girls would come into an open space between the trees onto a surprise batch of wildflowers.

"I hear the waterfall!" cried Samantha. She ran ahead of the others to a sunny clearing. And there it was, looking just exactly the way it did in her mother's painting: a lacy curtain of water splashing down giant steps of stones. The water spray caught the sun and made little rainbows. Samantha's heart thudded. It was the most beautiful thing she had ever seen.

Without a word, the three girls pulled off their shoes and stockings. They bunched up their skirts and waded into the shallow pool at the foot of the waterfall. They got as close to the fall as they could and let the spray mist their faces. The water was icy cold. It felt wonderful after their hot canoe ride.

"Next time we come, we'll have to bring our bathing suits," said Agnes.

Samantha grinned. "I don't mind getting wet," she said. She pulled off her middy blouse and skirt and walked straight into the waterfall in her chemise and drawers. Agatha was right behind her.

"Ooooh!" they shrieked with glee as the water showered them. "Come on in, Agnes! It's *freezing*!"

Agnes took off her blouse and skirt, folded them carefully, and began to walk slowly into the pool. Then, *oops*! She slipped on a mossy stone and fell, *plunk*!, on her bottom.

Samantha and Agatha laughed as they helped her stand up. "That's the fast way to get wet," Samantha giggled. She let the water pour down on her head and neck and shoulders until she couldn't stand the cold any longer. Then she ran out into the sunshine, and then back into the falls again.

After a while, the girls were cold down to their bones, so they stretched out on a warm rock to dry off. Samantha lay on her stomach and put her face into the water for a drink. "Oh!" she sputtered. "It's so cold, it makes my nose numb!"

Agnes nodded. "My skin is all tingly," she said. "And I'm hungry. Let's have our picnic."

They spread the picnic blanket on the rock and sat cross-legged, holding their big sandwiches in both hands.

"This is the nicest place I've ever been in my whole life," said Agatha.

"It's so peaceful," said Agnes. "All you can hear are water, birds, and the breeze."

"Now that you've seen the waterfall, do you remember coming here with your mother and father?" Agatha asked Samantha.

Samantha kicked one leg in the water, sending sparkling drops into the air. "I think so," she said slowly. "I feel as if I've been here before, but it's all mixed up. It's almost like dreaming."

"Well, it's a dreamy place," said Agnes. She tilted her face up to the sun. Water drops hung in her hair like pearls.

"I'm very glad your mother drew those pictures," said Agatha. "Otherwise we'd never have come here."

Samantha looked around. It gave her goose bumps to think that she was in a place she had been with her mother and father, and that nothing had changed. This very same rock and those very same trees were all in the pictures her mother had painted.

"Come on!" said Samantha, standing up. "Let's get dressed and explore. I want to find all the places my mother drew." She took her mother's sketchbook out of her pack basket.

"All right," agreed the twins.

The sketchbook was like a treasure map. It led the girls on a long, happy hunt. First they found the grassy field where Samantha and her parents used to have picnics. It was just as sunny as it looked in the picture Samantha's mother had painted.

The girls looked a long time before they found the big split rock that was in another picture. They found flowers growing in the shade of graceful white birch trees. The same flowers were in the picture that showed Samantha and her father picking a bouquet.

And finally, the girls climbed up to the highest point of the island so they could see the view. The dark green pines and the hills that sloped down to the wide lake looked the same as they did in the pictures Samantha's mother had painted.

"Gosh! You can touch the clouds up here!" said Agatha.

"Look, there's the goose's neck," said Agnes. She pointed to the narrow rocky part of the lake they had paddled through that morning.

"And there's Piney Point," said Samantha. "It looks very small from here."

The girls were so high up, they seemed to be standing where the sky met the land. The wind tugged at Samantha's skirt as if it wanted to lift her up like a kite into the clouds.

Samantha looked at the sky. The clouds were dark

and heavy. "I think we'd better go," she said to the twins. "It looks like it might rain."

Agatha squinted up at the clouds. "You're right," she said with a sigh. "But I hate to leave."

"We can come back," said Agnes.

"Oh yes," agreed Samantha. "We can always come back, anytime we want to."

They hiked back to the waterfall, gathered up their belongings, and put their pack baskets on their backs. Samantha felt tired but content as they walked down the narrow path to the lake shore. What a glorious day! She would remember it forever and ever. She was very glad they had come.

As the girls came to the edge of the water, the leaves of the silver maples were showing their shiny undersides. That was always a sign that a storm was coming.

"Is this where we left the canoe?" asked Agatha.

"I think so," said Samantha.

"Well, I don't see it," said Agatha.

"Uh-oh," said Agnes. The girls stood in a row on the pebbly shore.

"Didn't you tie it up?" Agatha asked Agnes.

"No!" Agnes wailed. "I thought you did."

"Well," said Samantha calmly, "it's probably just drifted off a little bit. Let's walk around the shore and see if it's washed up somewhere else."

It was very hard to walk around the shore of the island. The girls had to climb up and down big jagged rocks that were slippery from the lake spray. Soon all three girls were wet and out of breath. The canoe was nowhere in sight.

"I'm cold," complained Agnes. "What will we do now?"

"Swim home?" Agatha suggested desperately.

Samantha wished she could laugh, but Agatha's silly ideas didn't seem very funny now. "We have to use our heads," she said. "Let's go back up to the rocky cliff. We can see all around the island from up there. We're sure to spot the canoe."

Wearily, they trudged up the same hill that they'd scampered up just a few hours earlier. They followed the path past the waterfall and up to the rocky cliff. By now the sky was the color of tarnished silver and the wind was strong. Samantha held her wet hair in one hand to keep it from blowing in her face. She looked all around, but there was no canoe to be seen. No canoe at all. Samantha's stomach flopped with fear.

"We're stranded!" moaned Agatha. "How will we ever get back to Piney Point?"

"Someone will come and get us," said Samantha.

"But how will they know we're here?" asked Agnes.

"We could send smoke signals," said Agatha.

"But we don't have matches. How can we start a fire?" asked Samantha.

"Uh, you rub two sticks together, I think," said Agatha, uncertainly. "Or you can make paper catch fire with a magnifying glass. I read that in a book!" She pawed through her pack basket and dragged out her magnifying glass.

"It won't work. The sun's got to be shining," Samantha said. And the sun certainly was not shining at the moment. Big black clouds crowded next to each other, blocking the sun completely.

"Maybe if we made lots of noise, someone would hear us," said Agnes.

So Samantha blew on her bo's'n's whistle as hard as she could. Agnes and Agatha shouted, "Help! Help! Somebody help!" But the wind was blowing so hard, they knew no one could hear them.

"Jeepers, I'm hungry," said Agatha. "It must be dinnertime by now."

"Well, at least, when we're not home for dinner, they'll realize something is wrong," said Agnes. "In fact, they probably started looking for us when we weren't back to swim with the Admiral."

Samantha hoped Agnes was right. She sat down next to a big rock to get shelter from the wind. It was getting colder and colder. All three girls wrapped up together in the picnic blanket, but it didn't help much. It felt as if they sat there for hours, watching the sky get darker and darker. A chilling drizzle began to fall.

"We may have to sleep here tonight," said Agatha, hugging her knees to her chest.

Agnes shuddered. "I hope there are no wild animals to creep up on us."

Samantha started to say, "No, I don't think—" when they heard a rustling sound below them on the path.

"What's *that*?" Agatha cried.

"Shh!" hissed Agnes.

The girls heard more rustling. It might have been the wind, but it sounded more like a bear or a wolf, pushing through the trees, coming closer and closer. Then they heard a moan.

Samantha gasped.

"Eeek!" yelped Agnes. She clutched Samantha's arm. The girls held their breath and listened. The sounds came closer: another moan, more rustling, then a crash.

Samantha grabbed a big stick and stood up. "Get behind me," she whispered to Agnes and Agatha.

They heard the moan once more, and then a low voice struggling to be heard over the wind. "Help! Help me!"

Samantha lowered the stick. "Who's there?"

"Help!" the voice called again. "Oh! Samantha, help!"

The girls looked at each other, then started toward the voice, stumbling over one another as they headed down the hill. There, lying across the muddy path, was the Admiral!

"Oh, Admiral!" cried Samantha. She hurried toward him and knelt by his side. "What happened?"

The Admiral's voice was weak. "My head—it's my head . . ." he gasped. "I fell and hit it on the . . . on the . . . rocks." He put his hand up to his eye. In the darkness and rain, Samantha could just barely see the deep gash on his forehead and the blood that was trickling from it. The Admiral's eyelids drooped and he moaned again. "I came to . . . to help you," he whispered. "But now you'll have to help me." He tried to go on, but his voice failed, his eyes closed, and his head dropped onto the ground.

"Is he dead?" asked Agatha hoarsely.

Through the Passage

o," said Samantha. "I think he's unconscious." The Admiral's eyes were still closed.

"What will we do now?" wailed Agnes.

Samantha didn't want the twins to see how afraid she really was. She tried to act as if she knew just what to do. "Well," she said, "the first thing we have to do is to make him comfortable. Let's get him over to that rock where we ate lunch. The trees will give us a little shelter from the rain. We'll have to drag him."

Agnes took one of the Admiral's arms, and Samantha took the other. Very slowly, pulling with all their strength, the girls moved the Admiral over to the flat rock by the pool. The Admiral groaned, but he did not open his eyes.

"He needs a doctor," said Samantha. "We've got to

get him back to Piney Point as fast as we can."

"But how can we even get him to his boat?" asked Agnes. "He's too heavy to carry or drag all that way."

"We'll have to help him walk," said Samantha. She put her cold hand on the Admiral's forehead, then she shook his shoulder. "Admiral? Admiral, can you hear me?"

Slowly, he opened his eyes. Samantha and the twins gently helped him sit up. Then Samantha put one of his arms over her shoulder. Agnes took his other arm, and together they lifted him so that he was standing. He swayed for a moment, but then he steadied himself.

"Lean on us, Admiral," said Samantha. "We're going down to the boat."

The Admiral didn't say anything, but Samantha heard him take a deep breath. He tried to stand up straighter. His arm was heavy on Samantha's shoulder. Agatha gathered up all the pack baskets and led the way down to the shore. Agnes and Samantha struggled behind her, holding on to the Admiral's waist to steady him. The narrow path was slippery now because of the rain. Agnes and Samantha had to push wet branches out of the way with their free hands.

"That's it, that's good," Samantha murmured with every step. "You're doing fine, Admiral. Not much farther now."

The Admiral had left a lighted lantern in his boat. They headed toward it in the darkness. When they finally reached the boat, they helped the Admiral swing his legs over the side and lie down on the bottom. Samantha took a napkin from her pack basket, dipped it in the cold lake water, and laid it gently over the bloody cut on the Admiral's forehead. The girls covered him with their picnic blanket to help keep him warm.

"Girls . . ." the Admiral began. But his voice trailed off to nothing, and he closed his eyes again.

"All right," said Agatha in a wavery voice. "Let's go."

The three girls shoved the heavy rowboat into the water. The twins jumped in and sat side by side on the middle seat, each one taking an oar. Samantha knelt in the front, holding the lantern to light the way through the rain.

The Admiral's boat was much bigger and harder to handle than the canoe. The twins had to struggle against the wind and the choppy waves that slapped the sides of the boat. But they rowed slowly and steadily until they came to the narrow part of the lake where the rocks broke through the water.

"It's too narrow to row in here!" exclaimed Agatha.

"Use your oars to push off from the rocks," shouted Samantha.

The bottom of the heavy old boat scraped against rocks that were hiding beneath the water. On either side, boulders poked up out of the water like dark monsters. "Push right!" cried Samantha, then, "Right again. Hard!"

The boat rocked wildly from side to side, knocking against the boulders. Water splashed into the girls' faces and drenched their clothes. *It was probably like this the night my parents drowned,* Samantha said to herself. She shivered. Behind her, the Admiral stirred and groaned. *We've got to get through this passage,* Samantha thought. *We've got to get the Admiral back to Piney Point as soon as we can.*

Suddenly, the boat stopped with a hard *thud.* "We're stuck!" Agnes wailed. The front of the boat was caught between two big rocks. Samantha stood up and pushed against one of the rocks to get the boat free. She pushed so hard, she lost her balance and almost toppled out into the water. She steadied herself and pushed again, and finally the boat was free.

"Quick! Push hard to the left," Samantha yelled. After one more push they were out of the narrow passage, headed into the wide, black lake.

They had no time to catch their breath. The twins began to row again. They hunched over the oars, trying to keep the rain out of their eyes. They rowed as hard as they could, on and on, through the stormy darkness, across the lake that seemed as huge and endless as the ocean.

"Lights!" Samantha shouted at last. "I see lights! It's Piney Point!"

The twins twisted around to look at the welcome sight. In the main house at Piney Point, every lamp was lit. There were lights on the dock, and lights were bobbing in boats on the water.

"Grandmary! Uncle Gard!" Samantha yelled. "Help!" She waved the lantern back and forth and blew on her bo's'n's whistle again and again and again. Some of the lights seemed to be coming closer.

"I think they see us!" she called to the twins over

her shoulder. "I think they're coming!" She waved the lantern over her head. "Over here! Over here!" she shouted.

Out of the dark, she heard Uncle Gard call, "Samantha!" And suddenly, there he was in another boat alongside of them. "Samantha!" he said again. "Catch this rope. Tie it to the front of your boat. I'm going to haul you in."

"Hurry, Uncle Gard," Samantha said. "We've got the Admiral with us. He's hurt."

Uncle Gard tossed a heavy, wet rope to Samantha. She tied it to the front of the rowboat as well as she could. "All right," she called.

With a jolt and a thump, Uncle Gard's boat began to pull them toward Piney Point. The boats moved quickly, and in no time they were at the dock. In the jumble of voices and lights, Samantha didn't even know who lifted her out of the rowboat.

"Be careful!" she said as the men began to move the Admiral. "He's hurt. Watch his head." And then Grandmary was hugging her so hard, she could barely breathe.

"Oh my dear," murmured Grandmary. She

smoothed Samantha's hair away from her face. "Oh my dear. Thank God you're all right."

Together, Grandmary and Samantha climbed the steps up the hill. Samantha's legs were wobbly. She leaned against Grandmary and followed the path of lights to the main house. At last, she and the twins and the Admiral were all safe.

Later on, the three girls were sitting in front of the fire in the big room of the main house. Cornelia had given them all hot baths, rubbed them dry, and wrapped them in blankets. They sat quietly, sipping their cocoa, watching the doctor take care of the Admiral.

"You're a lucky fellow, Admiral," said the doctor. He wrapped a clean white bandage around the Admiral's forehead. "It's a good thing these girls got you home so quickly. This cut could have been very serious. How did it happen?"

"Well," said the Admiral, "when I saw the storm coming up, I set out to find the girls. They weren't on the lake nearby, so I knew they'd gone through the passage. I had a bit of a time getting past those rocks in the rowboat—"

"Oh, the rocks in that passage are terrible!" said Grandmary. "Especially in a storm!" Her face was pale.

The Admiral squeezed her hand to comfort her, then went on. "Once I was through, I heard your whistle, Samantha. Then I saw your canoe. It was partly sunk in the water near Teardrop Island. I suppose you didn't beach it properly."

The girls hung their heads.

"I realized you were stranded on the island, so I hurried to help you. I landed my boat and jumped out, but I slipped on the rocks and hit my head. After that, I don't remember much. I think I tried to find you. The next thing I knew, you were helping me into the boat. And then we were home, safe and sound at Piney Point."

The Admiral sat up in his chair as if it were a throne and his bandage were a crown. "I'm proud to know you girls," he said. He patted Samantha on the hand. "You really saved the day, young lady."

Grandmary sighed. "I was so worried about you,

all of you," she said. "I was so afraid. It was just like the night, that awful night . . ." She shook her head.

Samantha had never seen her grandmother look so weary. "I'm sorry we frightened you, Grandmary," she said. "I didn't mean to. I just had to go to Teardrop Island. I had to see the waterfall."

"You remembered the waterfall?" Grandmary asked. She looked surprised.

"No," answered Samantha. "I didn't remember it. I saw it in this book." She pulled the sketchbook out from the folds of her blanket.

"Lydia's sketchbook," said Uncle Gard softly. "I haven't seen that in years. Not since . . ." He didn't finish his sentence.

Samantha handed the book to Grandmary. "I didn't remember anything about Teardrop Island. I didn't know I had ever been there with my parents, until I saw this book," she said. "That's why I had to go there today. I wanted to see all the places on the island we used to go. I wanted to try to remember what it was like when we all went there together, as a family."

Grandmary stared down at the book in her lap. "You and your parents had many happy times on that island," she said. "You are right to try to remember."

"It all looks exactly the same, Grandmary," Samantha said. "Everything on the island is just as pretty as it is in my mother's drawings. It's a beautiful, happy place. I'd like to go back again." She looked up at Grandmary. "Maybe you'd like to come with me sometime."

"Perhaps I will," Grandmary said softly. "Perhaps I will."

Samantha *did* go back to Teardrop Island that summer, and Grandmary went with her. They visited the waterfall. They picked wildflowers. They had a picnic lunch on a shady hillside overlooking Goose Lake. They found the split rock that was in Samantha's mother's sketchbook. Together, Samantha and Grandmary made new memories of the place that had once meant so much to Samantha's parents.

At the end of the summer, Admiral Beemis asked Grandmary to marry him, just as he had done every summer before. This time, to everyone's surprise, Grandmary said yes!

Grandmary and the Admiral were married in New York City, and then they sailed away on the Admiral's yacht for a long honeymoon. Now Samantha did indeed have a grandfather who was great.

A New Home

When Grandmary and the Admiral left for their honeymoon, Samantha stayed in New York City with Uncle Gard and Aunt Cornelia. It was great fun to live with her aunt and uncle, and Samantha loved all the sights and sounds of the big city. She liked her new school and quickly made many friends. But Samantha missed her best friend, Nellie, who lived back in Mount Bedford.

Nellie, her parents, and her two sisters worked as servants in the home of Grandmary's neighbor, Mrs. Van Sicklen. Samantha had written a long letter to Nellie three weeks ago, but she hadn't gotten a reply yet.

Maybe there will be a letter from Nellie today, Samantha thought as she hurried along the city sidewalk. Her ice skates were slung over one shoulder. She was cold, so she pulled her hat down over her ears and then rubbed her hands together inside her snug fur muff. The sky was pink darkening to purple as she ran up the steps to Uncle Gard and Aunt Cornelia's house.

"Hello!" she called out as she pushed open the heavy door and came into the bright hallway. "I'm home!"

"There you are, dear," said Aunt Cornelia. She gave Samantha a hug. "I was afraid you'd frozen to the ice! It must have been awfully cold at the skating pond this afternoon. Come sit by the fire and have some tea. That will warm you up."

Samantha followed Aunt Cornelia into the cozy parlor. She sat by the fire and held her stiff hands up to the glow to melt the coldness away. This was Samantha's favorite time of the day. Every afternoon as dusk settled over the city, Samantha and Aunt Cornelia shared a pot of tea and chatted while they waited for Uncle Gard to come home from his office. This after-noon, Samantha noticed a big box on the tea table. A bit of silky pink ribbon was slipping out from under the lid. "What's in the box, Aunt Cornelia?" she asked.

"Valentines!" said Aunt Cornelia. She lifted the lid

and turned the box upside down. Out spilled loops of ribbon, paper lace doilies, tiny red hearts, and sheets of paper covered with pictures of cupids and flowers. "Saint Valentine's Day is only a few weeks away. I thought we'd better start making our valentines now, since—"

"We have so many to make this year!" Samantha finished eagerly. She picked up a pink ribbon and two hearts. "My first valentine will be for Grandmary and the Admiral."

"The newlyweds!" smiled Aunt Cornelia.

"I'll make two hearts joined together," said Samantha. "That seems right for people who just got married, doesn't it?"

"Yes, indeed," said Aunt Cornelia. She began cutting out pictures of cupids.

"Oh, it's so romantic," sighed Samantha. "I mean the way Grandmary and the Admiral finally got married after being so fond of each other for all those years."

"Mmm," agreed Aunt Cornelia.

"I'm sure they're happy, sailing around the world on the Admiral's yacht," said Samantha. "I do miss them both just terribly. But I'm glad I live here with you and Uncle Gard."

"We're glad, too!" smiled Aunt Cornelia.

Just then the parlor door opened. "Begging your pardon, madam," a cool voice interrupted. It was Gertrude, the housekeeper. She was carrying the tea tray. Samantha sat up a little straighter. Gertrude always made her feel as if she had done something wrong. Now Gertrude looked down her long nose at the messy tea table covered with bits of ribbon and paper. "And *where* shall I place the tray, madam?" she asked Aunt Cornelia.

"Oh, anywhere will do," said Aunt Cornelia. She didn't look up. She was busy pasting cupids onto paper lace doilies.

Gertrude didn't move.

"Just put it on Samantha's stool by the fire, Gertrude," said Aunt Cornelia. "Sam can sit on the floor."

"The *floor*, madam?" sniffed Gertrude.

"Yes," said Aunt Cornelia. "And Gertrude, would you mix up another batch of flour paste for us, please? We've used up this jar." She handed

Gertrude the sticky jar of paste.

If Aunt Cornelia had handed her a pail of snakes and hoptoads, Gertrude could not have looked more disgusted. She held the paste jar with the very tips of her fingers as she left the room.

Aunt Cornelia brought Samantha a cup of sweet, hot tea and looked down at the valentine Samantha had just finished. "Oh, how lovely!" she exclaimed. "Grandmary and the Admiral will love it!"

Samantha set the valentine carefully on a corner of the table. "Now I'll make one for Nellie," she said. "This one really has to be especially pretty because Nellie is my very best friend in Mount Bedford."

"You miss her a lot, don't you?" said Aunt Cornelia.

"Yes," said Samantha. "And I worry about her, too. She has to work very hard at Mrs. Van Sicklen's, and she's not very strong."

Aunt Cornelia sighed. "But Nellie is better off there than she would be here in the city."

"I know," said Samantha. "When Nellie lived in the city before, she worked in a terrible, dangerous factory. It was horrible."

"At least Nellie had a loving family to go home

to," said Aunt Cornelia. "Lots of children who work in those factories are orphans. The lucky ones live in orphanages. The others live on the streets."

Samantha shivered. She had seen many poor, raggedy children in the city. She was glad Nellie was safe with her family in Mount Bedford, even if she *was* far away. "Maybe we could make valentine cookies and send them to Nellie," said Samantha.

"What a good idea!" said Aunt Cornelia. "We'll make cookies for Nellie and Agnes and Agatha . . ."

"And Uncle Gard!" added Samantha. "It will be a surprise for him!"

"A surprise?" Uncle Gard poked just his head into the parlor. "Are my two best girls planning a surprise for me? Well, I've got a surprise, too," he said. He reached into the pocket of his coat and handed Samantha a postcard and a letter.

"Oooh, look!" said Samantha. "It's a postcard from Grandmary and the Admiral." She read aloud Grandmary's elegant, spidery script:

My dear Samantha,

The Admiral and I are sailing in the warm, blue-green waters off Greece! It's lovely! We're very happy, but we do miss our dear girl. Please give our love to your Uncle Gardner and Aunt Cornelia.

Ever your devoted
Grandmary

Ahoy matey)!
What ho! XOXO
Your
Admiral

Samantha laughed. "Look," she said. "The Admiral drew a picture for all of us." She handed the card to Uncle Gard and Aunt Cornelia and looked down at the letter in her lap. "Jiminy!" she exclaimed. "It's from Nellie!" She ripped open the envelope eagerly and began to read aloud.

"Dear Samantha, I am glad you are so happy living at your aunt and uncle's house. I am fine, but . . ."

Suddenly, Samantha stopped reading aloud because the words were too horrible. She read to herself:

I am fine, but I have some very sad
news. The flu has been very bad here
in Mount Bedford this winter. We all
had it except Jenny. My mother and
father died. I miss them so much. Mrs.
Van Sicklen says they are in heaven
where God will take care of them. Mrs.
Van Sicklen has been kind, but now we
must leave her house. Bridget and Jenny
and I are moving to New York City to live
with our Uncle Mike. I will come to see
you as soon as I can. I promise.

Your friend,
Nellie

"Oh, poor Nellie!" Samantha whispered. "Poor
Bridget and Jenny!"

"What is it, Samantha?" Aunt Cornelia asked.

Samantha couldn't talk. She was too afraid she
would cry. She handed the letter to Aunt Cornelia.

Aunt Cornelia and Uncle Gard read it together.
When they finished, Uncle Gard picked Samantha up
and held her on his lap. Aunt Cornelia took both her
hands.

"Sometimes," Aunt Cornelia said in a soft, slow
voice, "it's very hard to understand why such sad, sad
things happen to good people, people we love. Nellie
and her sisters are very young to be without their
parents. But they have their uncle, and I am sure he
will take care of them."

Uncle Gard cleared his throat. Samantha knew he
and Aunt Cornelia were both just as sad as she was.
"Nellie and her little sisters will be in New York, Sam.
They won't be far away anymore," he said. "We'll be
able to see them and be sure they're all right. Isn't that
so, Cornelia?"

Aunt Cornelia didn't answer, but she squeezed
Samantha's hands.

"Nellie says she'll come to see me when she gets to
New York," Samantha said. It was the one good thing
in the middle of the sadness—like one candle in a big,
dark room. "Nellie promised to come, so I know she
will. Oh, I hope she comes soon!"

Searching for Nellie

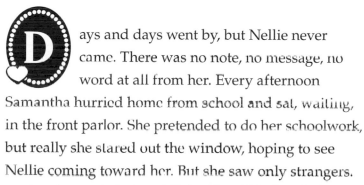

Days and days went by, but Nellie never came. There was no note, no message, no word at all from her. Every afternoon Samantha hurried home from school and sat, waiting, in the front parlor. She pretended to do her schoolwork, but really she stared out the window, hoping to see Nellie coming toward her. But she saw only strangers.

Her hopes faded as each bright afternoon faded into gray twilight. She read Nellie's letter over and over again, adding up the days in her head. One day for Nellie to pack, one day to travel, one day with her uncle . . .

Samantha began to worry. Maybe something had happened. Maybe Nellie was sick with the flu again. Maybe Mrs. Van Sicklen wanted her to stay in Mount Bedford. Or maybe her uncle wouldn't let her come to visit. Something had to be wrong, because if Nellie was in New York, Samantha knew that she would keep her promise.

The first few evenings, as soon as Uncle Gard came in the door, he asked about Nellie. "Did she come today, Sam?" But after a while, he didn't need to ask. He could tell the answer was no by the disappointed look on Samantha's face.

One night after dinner, Uncle Gard said, "Tonight we'll telephone Mrs. Van Sicklen and find out where Nellie and her sisters are."

"That's a good idea," said Aunt Cornelia.

"Telephone?" asked Samantha. "But it's all the way to Mount Bedford. That's long distance."

"What else do we have a newfangled contraption like the telephone for?" asked Uncle Gard.

Samantha and Aunt Cornelia followed Uncle Gard into the hallway and watched as he cranked the telephone. "Operator?" he shouted into the mouthpiece. "Hello? Operator? I want to speak to the Van Sicklen residence in Mount Bedford, please." Samantha heard some loud crackling on the line, and then Uncle Gard shouted, "Mrs. Van Sicklen, please.

Mrs. Van Sicklen? Gardner Edwards here. No, no, nothing's wrong. Sorry to alarm you by telephoning. We're wondering where Nellie is. Nellie, your little maid, and her sisters Bridget and Jenny."

Uncle Gard paused. Then his voice was serious. "Two weeks ago? I see. Well, do you happen to know their uncle's exact address? No? I don't suppose he has a telephone? No, no, I thought not. Well, thank you, Mrs. Van Sicklen. I'll ring off now." He turned the crank, hung up the earpiece, and looked at Samantha.

"Mrs. Van Sicklen says the girls left Mount Bedford two weeks ago. She put them on the train herself. The uncle's name is Mike O'Malley. Mrs. Van Sicklen didn't know his exact address, but she thinks he lives somewhere near the river, on 17th or 18th Street."

"They left Mount Bedford two weeks ago," repeated Samantha. "Why hasn't Nellie come to see me in all that time?"

"Nellie may be working," Uncle Gard said. "Or maybe she's too busy looking after Bridget and Jenny."

Samantha felt desperate. "Can't we try to find them? If we could just find where Nellie's uncle lives—"

"Samantha," Aunt Cornelia interrupted gently, "New York is a big place. It would be very hard— probably impossible—to find Nellie's uncle by just wandering around. I'm afraid all we can do is wait for Nellie to come to us."

"Don't give up hope, Sam," said Uncle Gard. "Nellie will come one of these days. I'm sure she will."

He tried to turn his worried frown into a smile, but Samantha could tell by his voice that Uncle Gard wasn't really sure Nellie *would* come. Samantha was quiet for a moment. She was thinking hard. Then she said, "Thank you for telephoning, Uncle Gard." She climbed up the stairs to her room. With each step, she was more determined. She didn't care how hard it would be. She was going to find Nellie. And she would go the very next day.

After school the next afternoon, Samantha set out under a heavy gray sky. She was more than a little nervous. In just a few blocks, she was in a part of the city she had never seen before. But she followed the street signs carefully and found 17th Street without any trouble. A strong wind at her back seemed to push her right to it.

But after she had walked toward the river for five or six blocks, 17th Street changed. Samantha had to jostle her way down the icy, muddy middle of the street because the sidewalks were blocked with pushcarts. The carts were piled high with potatoes, baskets, brooms, and buckets. The air was so full of the smell of fish and smoke, it seemed as dense as fog.

And there were so many people! Women dressed all in black with shawls over their heads poked at the things on the carts. Silent men stood next to small fires, rubbing their hands. Packs of raggedy-looking boys ran through the crowd.

Samantha began to feel as small and timid as a mouse in the hubbub around her. All the noise and strangeness was frightening. But she could not turn back. *It's a good thing there are so many people out on the street,* she said to herself bravely. *Someone here must know Nellie's uncle.*

But the cold that was chilling her hands and feet seemed to be freezing up her courage, too. When she saw steam rising from a cart of roasted chestnuts, she decided to get some because they looked so nice and hot.

Samantha handed the chestnut man a penny. As he gave her the bag of nuts, he said, "There you are, missy. The chestnuts will cheer ye. Put 'em in your muff to warm up your hands."

His singsong accent reminded Samantha of the way Nellie's father had talked. "Please, sir," she said. "Do you know Mr. O'Malley?"

The man grinned. "Sure and there are many, many O'Malleys, miss. Which one would you be wanting?"

"Mr. Mike O'Malley," said Samantha. "He lives on 17th or 18th Street."

The grin vanished from the man's face like a light blown out by a cold wind. "And what would a young missy such as yourself be wanting with a hooligan like Mike O'Malley?" he asked.

"My friend Nellie, his niece, is with him," said Samantha. "Please, do you know where he lives?"

The man thought for a moment, then said, "Last I heard he was living—if you can call it that—over on 18th Street, above the shoemaker."

"Thank you!" said Samantha.

"Mind you be careful!" warned the man as Samantha hurried away, the bag of chestnuts tucked in her muff.

She walked fast, but she was worried. Was Nellie's uncle a bad man? The chestnut man had called him a hooligan. Samantha was not sure what a hooligan was, but she was quite sure she did not want to meet one. Only the idea of finally seeing Nellie kept her going. By now she was expert at dodging people and carts. In no time she'd rounded the corner and found the shoemaker's shop on 18th Street. There, outside the shop, she stopped. She stood silently staring at the building.

Is this where Nellie lives? she wondered. The gloomy building was horrible. It was falling apart and looked as if it were too tired to stand up anymore. Tattered laundry hung from the windows like flags of defeat.

Samantha did not want to go in the dark doorway. Then she thought, *Maybe Nellie has to go in this doorway every single day. Maybe Nellie is inside there right now.*

She climbed the steps and went inside. The door slammed shut behind her as if the building were swallowing her whole. The hallway smelled like rotting garbage. It was so dark, Samantha could hardly see. She held her breath and started up the creaky steps. Suddenly, at the top of the steps, a door flew open and a woman stuck her head out.

"What do you want?" she asked in a hard voice.

Samantha froze. "I'm . . . uh, I'm looking for Mr. Mike O'Malley," she croaked.

"Hist!" frowned the woman. "You'll not find him here, I'm happy to say. Now go away!" She started to close the door.

"Please, ma'am," said Samantha. "I was told he lived here. I've got to find him. He's got Nellie, and . . ."

"Nellie?" asked the woman. She stopped closing the door. A little face appeared at her knees, peeking around her skirts, smiling at Samantha. The woman scooped up the baby and opened the door a bit wider. "Is it Nellie you're looking for?"

"Yes!" said Samantha.

The woman still didn't smile, but she said, "Come along in then! Quickly now!"

Samantha stepped inside. She stood awkwardly near the door in a small room. It was not much lighter than the hallway, but it was scrubbed clean. It was

more crowded than any room Samantha had ever seen.
It was everything at once. One part was a kitchen.
There were beds, and chairs pushed together to make
beds, in each corner. In the middle of the room there
was a wooden table where six children sat. They were
making flowers out of paper. They all looked up
shyly at Samantha, but their fingers never stopped
twisting the colorful paper onto wire stems. It seemed
odd to see the bright blossoms in the middle of the
dark, cheerless room.

"All right, children," said the woman kindly.
"Gawking won't get the work done faster, will it?" She
bounced the baby on her hip while she told her story.
"That Mike O'Malley," she said, as if the name were a
curse. "He did live here, and drinking was all he was
good for, you'll pardon me saying, miss. Then about
two weeks ago, the three girls came to live with him.
Good, polite girls they were, too. And if Mike O'Malley
didn't take all of their money, and anything else they
had, and run off! He left them all alone in that room
upstairs. They had nothing to eat and nowhere to sleep
but the bare floor. Well! The oldest one, that Nellie, was
as bright a child as I've ever seen. She tried to clean

up the place and make it decent, but they couldn't stay there with no coal for a fire and not two pennies to rub together."

The woman shifted the baby to her other hip and continued. "So I took them in here. They sat down to work, and there was never a word of complaint from one of them. But we're crowded in here already, as you can see. After about a week, Nellie said they couldn't stay and be eating our food any longer. So I did the only thing I knew to do. I took them to the orphanage, where at least they'll be safe and warm and fed and get some schooling. Aye, and didn't it break my heart to see them go."

"They're in an *orphanage*?" asked Samantha.

"Yes," said the woman. "Over on 20th Street. It's called Coldrock House for Homeless Girls." She shook her head. "They've got no one left in the world to care for them now, poor things. Though you mark my words, they're better off without that good-for-nothing uncle."

Samantha couldn't believe what she had heard. Nellie and the girls were in an orphanage! Coldrock House didn't sound very warm or welcoming. "Thank you," Samantha said to the woman. "Now I know where to find Nellie. Thank you for being so kind."

"It's the least I could do for the dear girls," said the woman. "If you see Nellie and the little ones, give them my best love and say I still think of them and wish I could do more for them myself."

Samantha shook the woman's hand. "I will," she said. "I'll tell them."

Then she turned and rushed down the steps, out into the steely gray dusk. She hurried home through the shadowy streets, thinking only of Nellie and her sisters

Coldrock House

amantha couldn't sleep that night. She pulled the blankets up to her nose, but above them her eyes were wide open. She listened to the swoosh and sigh of the sleet against her window. She heard the passing horses snort and stamp and jingle their harnesses to shake off the dreary cold. Mostly, she worried about Nellie. What kind of place was Coldrock House for Homeless Girls? Was Nellie all right there? Tomorrow she would see for herself.

The next morning at breakfast, Aunt Cornelia said, "You look tired, Samantha. Do you feel all right?"

"Oh yes, I'm fine," said Samantha. "I just . . . I just didn't sleep too much last night."

Uncle Gard's face wrinkled with concern. "Now, Sam," he said, "I know you're worried about Nellie and the little ones. I am, too. It's hard not really knowing how they are, or even exactly where they are."

"I do know exactly where they are," Samantha said quietly.

"You do?" asked Uncle Gard and Aunt Cornelia together.

Samantha nodded. "Nellie and Bridget and Jenny are in an orphanage. It's called Coldrock House for Homeless Girls. It's on 20th Street."

Uncle Gard and Aunt Cornelia were silent.

"I know because I went to Nellie's uncle's house yesterday," Samantha went on. "And a neighbor told me about Nellie."

Uncle Gard and Aunt Cornelia looked at each other. Then Uncle Gard said, "Samantha, you went to a dangerous part of the city. Don't go there again. Do you understand?"

"Yes," said Samantha. "I'm sorry. I just had to try to find Nellie and the girls. And now I know where they are. At Coldrock House."

"Samantha, I'll go to Coldrock House with you this afternoon," said Aunt Cornelia. "They might not allow you in if you're by yourself."

"Thank you!" said Samantha. She smiled for the

first time that morning.

Aunt Cornelia smiled back. "We'll pack a small valise for Nellie and her sisters," she said. "I'm sure they could use some warm clothes."

"Yes! And books," said Samantha. "Nellie loves books, and pens and paper and . . ."

"Cookies!" exclaimed Uncle Gard. "And sweets!"

Samantha laughed. "You're right, Uncle Gard," she said as she hugged him. She knew he was relieved to know where Nellie and her sisters were, too.

It was biting cold that afternoon when Samantha and Aunt Cornelia walked to Coldrock House. Samantha followed her aunt up the steps to the stern, unwelcoming building, which looked as if it had been built out of blocks of dirty gray ice. It was surrounded by a fence of sharp black spikes. Samantha couldn't tell if the spikes were meant to keep visitors *out* or the orphans *in*. Samantha hated to think of Nellie and her sisters living *here*.

A pale, pinched-looking maid opened the door when Aunt Cornelia knocked. "Would you announce me to the directress?" Aunt Cornelia said. "I'm Cornelia Edwards, and this is my niece, Samantha Parkington."

Without a word, the maid led them to a dark, cold parlor. It was very, very quiet. Samantha couldn't believe the building had children in it. Didn't any of them make a noise?

Suddenly, soundlessly, a stout woman appeared. She was frowning. When she saw Aunt Cornelia and Samantha, her eyes narrowed for a moment. She studied her two well-dressed guests, and then she smiled a fake smile. Her eyes widened with put-on delight. "How perfectly lovely," she exclaimed, holding her hand out to Aunt Cornelia. "Mrs. Edwards! Miss Parkington! How nice of you to visit us! I'm Tusnelda Frouchy, the directress here at Coldrock House. Please sit down. And how may I help you? Have you come to hire a maid or a serving girl?"

"Not today," replied Aunt Cornelia. "We've come to see Nellie O'Malley."

Miss Frouchy looked surprised. Her sickly-sweet smile faltered for a moment, then spread itself wide again. "That's impossible," she said. "Our girls have visitors on Sunday afternoons only, from three to four o'clock. That's the rule. I'm sorry." She didn't sound sorry at all.

"This is a special case," Aunt Cornelia said firmly. "Nellie is a dear friend of my niece's. We haven't seen her in a long time. I'm sure you understand."

Miss Frouchy patted Samantha's cheek. Her puffy hands were soft but very, very cold. Samantha did not think she liked Miss Tusnelda Frouchy.

"I had no idea Nellie had such perfectly lovely friends," Miss Frouchy said. She turned to the maid and snapped, "Get her." While they waited, Miss Frouchy went on. "Nellie and her sisters are new here at Coldrock House, and of course, they're still a bit . . . a bit independent-minded, shall we say. But they'll adjust, I'm sure. Our girls quickly learn the rules here: Obedience. Order. Discipline—"

"Nellie!" cried Samantha. She jumped out of her chair and ran to hug her friend. "Nellie! I'm so glad to see you!"

"Samantha?" Nellie didn't seem to believe her eyes. "Oh, Samantha! You're here!" Nellie's face was full of joy.

"I was so worried when you didn't come to Uncle

Gard and Aunt Cornelia's," said Samantha. "I even
went to your uncle's house to find you and Bridget and
Jenny."

"You didn't!" gasped Nellie. Her eyes were wide.
"How did you ever—"

"Nellie!" Miss Frouchy interrupted. Her voice was
very sharp.

Samantha felt Nellie stiffen. "Yes, Miss Frouchy,"
Nellie said.

"We haven't forgotten our manners, have we? Say
'how do you do' to Mrs. Edwards." Miss Frouchy
turned to Aunt Cornelia. "You'll have to forgive her."
She sighed. "Good manners are an important part of
Coldrock House training, but these rough girls come
to us without any idea of polite behavior at all." She
held up her hands helplessly.

Now Samantha was sure she didn't like Miss
Frouchy. Imagine calling Nellie rough! She could feel
her face grow red with anger. But she bit her tongue
as Nellie curtsied and murmured, "How do you do,
Mrs. Edwards."

"Nellie, dear," Aunt Cornelia said kindly, "we're so
very sorry about your parents—"

"Such a sad thing!" interrupted Miss Frouchy. She shook her head and pursed her lips, pretending to feel sympathy.

"Do you and Bridget and Jenny need anything?" Aunt Cornelia asked Nellie.

Before Nellie could answer, Miss Frouchy exclaimed, "Oh, nothing at all! They have warm clothes, good food, and a roof over their heads. They're learning how to make their way in the world as servants. But most important of all, they're learning to be grateful to their betters and to be obedient, hard-working girls." She turned to Nellie and asked, "Isn't that so, Nellie?"

"Yes, Miss Frouchy, ma'am," said Nellie, looking down at the floor.

Samantha studied Nellie while Miss Frouchy made a long speech about what a fine place the orphanage was. Nellie's hair was chopped short. Her drab brown dress was much too big. It was made out of scratchy material as rough as a potato sack. Nellie looked smaller and thinner than ever. Miss Frouchy said she was getting good food, but Samantha could see she definitely wasn't getting *enough* of it.

"Nellie," she said in a quiet voice, hoping Miss Frouchy wouldn't hear. "Look. We brought some things for you and Bridget and Jenny. We brought books and clothes and socks." Samantha began to unpack the valise. "We even brought some gingerbread, and—"

Suddenly, Miss Frouchy pounced like a tiger and snatched the things away. "I'll keep these for Nellie," she said. "We don't want the girls eating too much rich food. It's not good for them. And we don't want to spoil them with gifts. It makes them selfish. Isn't that right, Nellie?"

Nellie looked at Samantha helplessly.

"Isn't that right, Nellie?" Miss Frouchy hissed. Her green eyes were narrowed.

"Yes, Miss Frouchy, ma'am," Nellie answered.

Samantha didn't know what to do. She couldn't talk to Nellie with Miss Frouchy there. Luckily, Aunt Cornelia understood. "Miss Frouchy," she said, "would you be kind enough to give me a tour of Coldrock House? I'm so interested in your work here."

Miss Frouchy seemed to puff up with pleasure and pride. "Why, of course," she said. "Do come with me."

Aunt Cornelia smiled and winked at the girls as she

followed Miss Frouchy from the room.

"Jiminy! That Miss Frouchy is terrible!" exclaimed Samantha when she and Nellie were alone. "I just know she'll eat that gingerbread all by herself."

Nellie grinned, and suddenly she looked like her old self.

"Oh, Nellie," Samantha said. "Are you really, really all right?"

"It's not so bad here," said Nellie. "At least we're together. That's the most important thing of all."

"Are Bridget and Jenny all right?" asked Samantha.

Nellie's grin faded. "Well, Bridget's not strong, and Miss Frouchy thinks she's lazy and scolds her terribly. I try to do Bridget's work for her, but it's hard to fool Miss Frouchy. She's everywhere! She's as sneaky as a cat."

Samantha squinted her eyes and made a catty face like Miss Frouchy's. "Perfectly lovely!" she mimicked.

Nellie tried to hide her giggles behind her hand.

Samantha sighed. "I wish you three could come to live with Uncle Gard and Aunt Cornelia and me," she said.

"No," said Nellie. "They've got all the maids

they need. They don't want us."

"Well then, you could run away from here and *hide* at Uncle Gard and Aunt Cornelia's!" said Samantha. "They'd never know. You could stay in the attic, and I could take care of you and bring you food and everything—"

"Samantha," interrupted Nellie, "you know that would never work. If we ran away, we'd be caught and punished—really punished." Nellie looked very serious. "The best thing we can do is to stay here. They're training me to be a maid. Pretty soon they'll find a job for me, and I'll be able to work and take care of Bridget and Jenny."

"But—" Samantha began.

"Don't you see?" said Nellie. "All we've got is one another. Bridget and Jenny and I *have* to stay together. That's all that matters."

Samantha knew she could not change Nellie's mind. "Can you at least come visit Uncle Gard and Aunt Cornelia and me?"

"No," said Nellie. "Miss Frouchy wouldn't let us. But you can visit us here on Sundays."

"Only for an hour, and with that grouchy Miss

Frouchy watching us," said Samantha. "Oh, well," she sighed. "It's better than nothing. And I can bring you things, lots of things, like—" Just then Miss Frouchy came back into the room, so the girls had to stop talking. She hardly let them say good-bye before she sent Nellie away.

Aunt Cornelia was very quiet on the walk home. Samantha could tell she had not liked what she had seen of Coldrock House. All she said was, "Those poor children." She shook her head and put her arm around Samantha's shoulder to hold her close by her side.

In the Alley

U ncle Gard, Aunt Cornelia, and Samantha were waiting outside Coldrock House at exactly five minutes before three o'clock the next Sunday afternoon. They didn't want to miss a second of their visiting hour with Nellie, Bridget, and Jenny. They were all quite cheerful when they arrived, but they left feeling sad.

All the way home, Uncle Gard fussed and fumed about the way Miss Frouchy treated the girls. He had spent the hour talking to Bridget and Jenny. He had kept a serious expression on his face, hoping to fool Miss Frouchy into thinking he was quizzing the girls on the multiplication tables. But really he was asking them, "Miss Bridget O'Malley, where did you get those wonderful curls?" and "Miss Jenny O'Malley, how did you make your eyes such a pretty blue?" Bridget and

Jenny tried to answer him just as seriously, but once in a while they'd break out into giggles. Whenever they did, they looked nervously at Miss Frouchy. She would narrow her eyes and frown at them. And when Uncle Gard tried to give them some sweets, Miss Frouchy grabbed them away.

Samantha and Nellie talked as much and as fast as they could, but one hour was nowhere near enough time. At the end of the visit, Samantha asked Nellie in a whisper, "Can't we meet secretly? What if I sneak over here in the middle of the night when everyone is asleep? I can tap on your window, and you can climb out."

Nellie laughed. "I have a better idea. What if you came in the afternoon, on your way home from school? It's my job to empty the ashes from the fireplaces. I bring them to the ash cans in the alley out back every afternoon about four o'clock. Could you come then?"

"Oh, of course!" said Samantha.

So every afternoon after school, Samantha hurried off to visit Nellie at Coldrock House. Samantha had to be very careful to get there by four o'clock. If she was even five minutes late, she didn't see Nellie at all.

Even though they met almost every afternoon, it

never seemed that the girls had enough time together.
While they talked, Samantha emptied the ashes into
the cans so that Nellie had time to eat the food Samantha brought her. Nellie always looked hungry and tired
and pale. Samantha noticed her friend's hands were red
and chapped from the cold, so she gave Nellie her gloves.
But the next afternoon, Nellie wasn't wearing them.

"Why aren't you wearing the gloves?" Samantha
asked.

Nellie looked sorry. "Miss Frouchy took them," she
said.

"That old cat!" exclaimed Samantha. "Didn't you
tell her they were yours?"

"Yes," said Nellie, "but when I wouldn't tell her
where I got them, she said I must have stolen them."

"Stolen them!" sputtered Samantha. "*She* stole them
from *you*! I'd like to march right inside and take those
gloves away from Miss Tusnelda Frouchy."

"Samantha, don't," Nellie warned. "If Miss Frouchy
knew we were meeting, she'd be awfully mad. She'd—"

"Punish you?" Samantha finished for her.

Nellie nodded.

"Did she punish you for the gloves?"

Nellie nodded again. "No dinner," she said.

Samantha frowned. "From now on I'll bring more food instead of things like gloves. You can eat it right away or give it to Bridget and Jenny."

"That would be much better," said Nellie.

"I'll bring as much food as I can sneak past Gertrude," Samantha promised. "She's our stingy housekeeper. She's already noticed I seem to need more food than I ever did before. It won't be easy, so don't you let fat old Miss Frouchy get any of it!"

"Don't worry," grinned Nellie. "We'll eat it so fast, she'll never get a whiff of it!"

As the days went by, the afternoons seemed to be getting softer. The sun was still as pale as a pearl, but every day more light found its way to the narrow alley behind Coldrock House where Nellie and Samantha met. Then one afternoon, Nellie seemed much quieter than usual. She hardly seemed to hear Samantha's questions, and she put the apples Samantha brought in her apron pocket without even looking at them.

"What's the matter, Nellie?" Samantha asked at last.

"Has Miss Frouchy been punishing you again?"

"No," said Nellie.

"Then what?" asked Samantha.

Nellie slammed the lid onto the ash can so loudly, it made Samantha jump. "They've picked me to go on the orphan train," said Nellie.

"What's *that*?" asked Samantha.

"It's a train that goes out West. It's full of orphans from the city. The train stops in lots of little farm towns. People in the towns choose orphans to live with them and to work for them," Nellie explained.

Samantha was horrified. "But Nellie, you *can't* leave New York!"

"I don't have any choice," Nellie said. "Miss Frouchy says I have to go. I'm trained enough now, and I'm old enough to work. Farm people might want me."

"What about Bridget and Jenny?" Samantha asked.

"They're too young to go," Nellie said softly. "They'll stay here."

"Oh, no," said Samantha. "You'll be separated."

"Yes," said Nellie. Her eyes filled with tears.

"Nellie, we can't let that happen," Samantha said. "You and Bridget and Jenny may never see one another again." She looked Nellie square in the eyes. "Now you've *got* to run away. You've *got* to come to Uncle Gard and Aunt Cornelia's house and hide. Just for a while, just until we think of something else to do. Please, Nellie, please say you'll come."

Nellie thought for a moment. "If I could look for work while I was there . . ."

"Oh, yes!" said Samantha. "You can go out every morning and come back in at night. No one will see you. I'll be sure of that. And I'll be sure you have food and blankets and everything you need."

Nellie sighed. "It's not a very practical plan," she said. "It won't work for long, but it's our only choice."

"Then you'll do it?" asked Samantha.

Nellie smiled a little smile. "I guess so," she said. "We might as well try."

Samantha hugged Nellie hard. "Good!" she said. "Bring Bridget and Jenny with you tomorrow afternoon at four."

"All right," said Nellie. "I'll find a way."

"Don't worry," said Samantha. "I'll plan everything. This will be your last night at Coldrock House."

"I hope so," said Nellie. "I certainly hope so."

The next day after school, Samantha ran to Coldrock House so fast, she was there way too early. She waited next to the ash cans, hopping from one foot to the other, filled with nervous jitters. When the loud bell rang at four o'clock on the dot, Samantha stood perfectly still. It felt like forever, but it was really only a minute or two before Nellie, Jenny, and Bridget appeared. The two little girls looked so confused and fearful, Samantha tried to calm them.

"Everything will be all right," she said, though she was nervous, too. Samantha handed Nellie, Bridget, and Jenny shawls and scarves to cover up their orphan uniforms. "So no one will notice us," she explained.

With shaking, fumbling hands, Samantha and Nellie hurriedly helped Bridget and Jenny wrap themselves up. Just then, *CRASH!* One of the ash cans fell over. All four girls froze in fear. They heard a door open.

"Who's out there?" someone shouted.

"Run fast!" hissed Samantha. She and Nellie herded Bridget and Jenny ahead of them and ran, their hearts beating hard, as fast as they could run away from Coldrock House. "Hurry!" Samantha urged the girls breathlessly. "Hurry!"

They didn't slow down until they were near Uncle Gard and Aunt Cornelia's house. Jenny trotted along next to Samantha trustfully. It made Samantha feel very grown-up—like a big sister—to have Jenny relying on her so completely. She held Jenny's hand very tightly.

Samantha led the way to the alley behind the house. "We'll have to climb in this window to the basement storage room," she explained in a soft voice. "The back stairs start in the basement and go all the way up to the top floor. When we get inside, we'll take our shoes off so that no one will hear us. There's a door that leads to the kitchen right off the stairs, so be very quiet when we pass it. Gertrude may be in the kitchen. She notices everything and she's kind of mean, so just follow me and don't talk. Ready?"

Nellie, Jenny, and Bridget nodded. Samantha climbed through the small window into the dark basement, then reached up to help Jenny through. When they were all inside, Samantha tiptoed to the stairs and started up.

In the Alley

There was a lot of noise in the kitchen. Gertrude seemed to be banging pots and pans together, and the laundry wringer was going *thump, thump, thump*.

As quietly as whispers, the four girls climbed the steps up to the main floor, up past the bedroom floor, and up to the very top floor. Samantha put her finger to her lips and slowly opened the door at the top of the stairs. She peeked her head out and looked around. No one was there. She motioned the three girls to follow her, and they quickly darted into the empty room across the hall.

They all sighed with relief. "Phew!" said Samantha. "I've been holding my breath ever since we climbed in the window. I was about to burst!"

"Me, too!" said Nellie. She looked around the room. Winter sunshine made bright yellow patches of warmth on the faded rug. Samantha had brought up lots of her books and toys, and Jenny and Bridget sat right down and started to play with Samantha's pretty paper dolls. Nellie smiled when she saw the blackboard they used to have in the Mount Better School. "Everything looks very nice," she said to Samantha. "Thank you."

"It's a little cold up here," said Samantha. "I brought

up all the extra blankets I could find. Gertrude's room is right down the hall. You'll have to be very quiet when she's up here. I hope you will be all right."

"We'll be fine," Nellie said cheerfully.

Jenny and Bridget were hungry, so Samantha showed them the box of fruit and bread and cheese she'd smuggled up to the room. They both took apples. "I couldn't bring very much," Samantha explained. "Gertrude keeps an eagle eye on the food in this house. But don't worry. I'll find a way to bring more next time."

"Nellie," Jenny asked as she ate her apple, "do we have to go back to Miss Frouchy at the orphanage tonight?"

"No," said Nellie. "We're going to stay here."

Jenny looked glad. "Does that mean we're not orphans anymore?"

"Well . . ." Nellie began.

Samantha knelt down and put her hand on Jenny's shoulder. "You and Bridget and Nellie are still together," she said. "And you'll never be orphans as long as you have one another."

"And good friends like Samantha," added Nellie.

Together

or the next few days, Samantha felt as if she lived in two different worlds. In one world, she made valentines and cookies with Aunt Cornelia. She went to school, practiced her ice skating, and joked with Uncle Gard, just as usual. The other world was smaller and quieter, but just as happy. That world was hidden away upstairs, in the room where her secret family lived. Samantha was a very important member of that family. It was up to her to be sure that Nellie, Bridget, and Jenny had food to eat, water for drinking and washing, books to read—everything they needed.

Every morning before dawn, Nellie crept down the back stairs, climbed out the cellar window, and went about the city looking for work. She was gone all day. Bridget and Jenny stayed in the attic, playing with

paper dolls, napping, and whispering quietly together.
After their horrible days with their uncle and at the
orphanage, they were happy to stay safe and cozy in
their secret hideaway. And Nellie was always glad to
get back to them at the end of the day.

Samantha loved being with Nellie again, and she
liked being a big sister to Bridget and Jenny. Whenever
she could manage it, she slipped away to be upstairs
with her secret sisters. It was easy for Samantha to
keep them happy and amused. They all loved to hear
her tell about Aunt Cornelia and Uncle Gard. They
asked hundreds of questions. What color dress was
Aunt Cornelia wearing today? What did Uncle Gard
say when Samantha got an A on a spelling test? Did
Aunt Cornelia finish the valentines she was making?
What did they look like? When were Aunt Cornelia
and Samantha going to give Uncle Gard his valentine?
The three girls listened to everything Samantha said
with glowing eyes.

"Well," said Jenny one day, "I think your Aunt
Cornelia and Uncle Gard are the finest lady and gentle-
man in New York City!"

"Yes!" agreed Bridget. "The only thing I liked at

Coldrock House was when they visited. Once your Uncle Gard gave me a peppermint and Miss Frouchy didn't see," she remembered. "I made that peppermint last a long, long time. I wish I could have another one *right now*."

"I wish you could, too," sighed Samantha.

She was having a hard time finding enough food for the hungry girls. Samantha gave them most of her lunch, all of her afternoon snack, and anything else she could smuggle from the pantry. One day she bought bread at the bakery and hurried home with the loaf hidden under her plaid cape. Another day she tried to bring a pot of cocoa to the girls. Bridget was catching a cold, and Samantha wanted her to have something warm to drink. But Gertrude stopped her at the kitchen door.

"Where are you going with that pot of cocoa?" Gertrude asked sharply.

"Up—upstairs," said Samantha.

"I won't have chocolate spilled all over your bedroom," said Gertrude. "Sit here at the kitchen table and drink it. Though I do not understand why you need to drink a whole pot of cocoa," she scolded. "I've never seen a child eat and drink as much as you have lately. Glass after glass of milk! Tea cakes and sandwiches all the live-long day! All the fruit from the bowl in the dining room! The way food disappears in this house, you'd think we had ten children living here instead of just one."

Samantha gulped her cocoa. Gertrude was getting suspicious!

So the next evening, when Samantha sneaked into the pantry, she tried to be very, very careful. Quietly, she opened the cookie jar. Quietly, she took three of the heart-shaped cookies she and Aunt Cornelia had made. She wanted to have a little party for Nellie, Bridget, and Jenny because the next day was Valentine's Day. She put the cookies in her pocket, turned to go, and there was Gertrude!

Gertrude blocked the doorway, her hands on her hips. "Cookies?" she snapped. "You just had dinner!" She frowned at Samantha. "Are you keeping a pet in this house? Is there some animal up in the attic? Is that what you are feeding?"

"Oh, no!" said Samantha nervously.

"All week I've heard scratches and scurrying up

there at night when I'm in bed," said Gertrude. "There's *something* up there. I don't know whether it's mice or thieves or ghosts, but I'll find out sooner than soon!"

Samantha hurried away with her cookies. *She* knew what Gertrude was hearing. She'd have to warn the girls—and fast.

As soon as she was out of Gertrude's sight, she ran up the stairs. "You're going to have to be quieter than ever," Samantha panted to Jenny and Bridget. "Gertrude said she hears noises. And Nellie, maybe you'd better not go in and out for a few days. I'm afraid she may catch you on the stairs."

Nellie agreed sadly. "I haven't had any luck finding work anyway," she said. "No one wants me for a maid. They think I don't look strong enough." She sounded discouraged. "I think I'll probably have to go back to the thread factory where I worked before we moved to Mount Bedford."

"Don't give up yet, Nellie," said Samantha. "It's only been a few days."

"I know," said Nellie. "But we can't stay here forever."

Samantha knew Nellie was right. But she didn't know what to do.

Then, suddenly, the door flew open and Gertrude stormed in! "Whatever is going on here?" she demanded. "Who are these children? What are they doing here? What have you been up to, Miss Samantha?"

Samantha couldn't think of anything at all to say. She just sat there miserably.

"Well!" said Gertrude with a smirk. "I think you'd better come with me. And these ragamuffins had better come, too. Just wait till your aunt and uncle see this! You certainly have some explaining to do, young lady! Now get downstairs."

Gertrude crossed her arms on her chest and glared at the girls as they filed slowly past her and down the stairs. Samantha's heart sank with every step she took. Her plan had failed. Now the girls would have to go back to Coldrock House. They'd have to face Miss Frouchy and punishment for running away. Worse than that, now they would be separated—probably forever. Nellie would be sent away on the orphan train.

Gertrude followed the girls into the parlor where Uncle Gard and Aunt Cornelia were sitting by the fire. When they saw Nellie and her sisters, they both gasped. "Why, Nellie! Bridget, Jenny! What are you doing here?" asked Aunt Cornelia.

"Begging your pardon, madam," said Gertrude, her eyes bright with self-importance. "These ragamuffins were hiding in your attic. Street children! No better than beggars! They've probably been sneaking through your house stealing from you!"

"That's not true!" burst out Samantha. "They'd never take anything!"

"Then who's been stealing all the food?" asked Gertrude.

"I have," said Samantha. She was so mad, she was almost crying. "*I'm* the thief, not them!"

"Now, let's calm down," said Uncle Gard. "Perhaps Samantha can explain all this."

"Well," she began. But just then Bridget sneezed.

"First, you'd better come sit here and get warm," Aunt Cornelia said gently. The four girls sat on the floor in front of the fire.

Samantha began again. "It's my fault. Nellie didn't want to run away from the orphanage. But Miss Frouchy was going to send her away on the orphan train. Bridget and Jenny were too young to go, so they would have had to stay at Coldrock House. They would never have seen Nellie again. So I talked Nellie into coming here, just until she could find a job where they could all be together."

"How long have they been here?" asked Aunt Cornelia.

"About four days," said Samantha.

"Four days!" exclaimed Aunt Cornelia. "But how did they eat?"

"I brought them food," said Samantha. "Gertrude is wrong. They'd never steal."

"I know that's true," said Aunt Cornelia. Uncle Gard didn't say anything. He just stared at the four sad girls.

Aunt Cornelia looked at him. "Well, Gardner," she said. "This is a very serious matter. What do you think we should do with these girls?"

"Give them warm baths and put them to bed," said Uncle Gard firmly. "We can decide the rest in the morning."

And that is exactly what they did. That night, Nellie, Bridget, and Jenny slept in Samantha's room.

This is probably the last time we'll be together, thought
Samantha as she watched the girls sleeping. Their faces
were pink and peaceful in the firelight.

Late into the night, Samantha heard low murmurs
coming from Uncle Gard and Aunt Cornelia's room.
She knew they were deciding what to do with Nellie
and Bridget and Jenny. Would they send them back
to Coldrock House? Would they let them stay for just
a little while longer? Would they try to find Nellie's
uncle? Finally, Samantha couldn't wonder or worry
any longer. She fell asleep.

The next morning when the girls came downstairs,
there were three more places set at the breakfast table.
And at every place there was a big red heart trimmed
with lace.

"Happy Valentine's Day, girls," said Aunt Cornelia.

"Happy Valentine's Day," they all replied.

"Let's have breakfast," Uncle Gard said cheerfully.

The four girls sat down. But before she could
swallow a crumb, Samantha's curiosity made her burst
out, "Uncle Gard, Aunt Cornelia, have you decided?

What are you going to do about Nellie and Bridget and Jenny? Couldn't they please stay here? They wouldn't be any trouble, and they'd be a big help around the house. They've all been taught to be maids . . ."

"We don't need any more maids," said Aunt Cornelia.

Samantha's heart sank.

"But we do need more girls here," said Uncle Gard. "I'd say we need three more girls, in a variety of sizes: tiny, medium, and still not very big." He turned to Nellie. "Miss Nellie O'Malley, how would you and Bridget and Jenny like to stay here? You could be sisters to Samantha and daughters to Cornelia and me."

Nellie looked very serious. "We would like it very, very much," she answered.

"Hurray!" shouted Samantha. She bounced out of her chair and ran to hug Aunt Cornelia, then Nellie, Bridget, and Jenny. Then all four girls hugged Uncle Gard and showered him with kisses.

"Well," smiled Uncle Gard, "what a lovely Valentine's Day this turned out to be! I have *five* of the sweetest valentines anyone could ever have. I must be the luckiest person in the world!"

Samantha laughed. "No, Uncle Gard," she said. "*I'm* the luckiest person in the world. At last, at last, I have a real family of my own!"

INSIDE Samantha's World

At the start of the twentieth century, Americans saw the world changing around them. Cities were getting bigger. Buildings were getting taller. Cars were taking the place of horses. More and more children—rich and poor, boys and girls—were able to go to school until they were sixteen. Education helped young women get jobs and earn money to take care of themselves.

When Grandmary was young, it wasn't proper for young ladies to even talk about money, and they certainly couldn't think about earning it! They were expected to live at home with their families until they got married and had husbands to take care of them. But by the time Samantha was old enough to work, people's attitudes had begun to change. Women could get jobs in department stores or in offices as secretaries. Many women became phone operators, since more and more homes and offices had telephones.

Even though women could finally have jobs and earn their own money, it still wasn't proper for them to live alone. So there were special women's hotels and boarding houses where America's "working girls" could live and be carefully *chaperoned*, or looked after.

Once a young woman like Samantha got married, she quit her job, moved to a home of her own, and began to raise a family. Her home, like most in America, would have many "modern" inventions. Even people who were not wealthy had electric lamps, running water, gas stoves, refrigerators, and washing machines. Samantha would have needed these new machines to make housework easier because it was hard to find people who wanted to be servants. The immigrants who used to fill the jobs of servants had gotten better jobs, so a woman like Samantha had to do many chores herself.

Since there were few servants willing to take care of elaborate clothes like the ones women wore in the early 1900s, fashions began to change, too. New styles were simpler to take care of and easier to wear. Back when Grandmary was a young woman, her long skirts and petticoats might have weighed as much as 25 pounds. Young women like Cornelia raised their hemlines a bit and stopped squeezing themselves into tight corsets that made it hard to move and even to breathe. By the time Samantha was a young woman, skirts were even shorter and clothing was even looser. These new styles upset some people. There were even laws that said women would have to pay a fine and go to jail if their skirts were more than three inches above the ankle!

But women liked the new freedom that shorter, more comfortable clothing gave them. These new styles seemed to be signs of the way women thought about themselves— as active people who had places to go and work to do. They were women who would not be hemmed in by old-fashioned clothing or old-fashioned attitudes.

Read more of SAMANTHA'S stories,
available from booksellers and at *americangirl.com*

✤ *Classics* ✤
Samantha's classic series, now in two volumes:

Volume 1:
Manners and Mischief
Making friends with a servant isn't proper for a young lady—but that won't stop Samantha!

Volume 2:
Lost and Found
Samantha finally finds her friend Nellie—living in an orphanage! She's determined to help Nellie escape.

✤ *Journey in Time* ✤
Travel back in time—and spend a day with Samantha!

The Lilac Tunnel
What is it really like to live in Samantha's world? What if you're a servant rather than a proper young lady? Find out by choosing your own path through this multiple-ending story.

✤ *Mysteries* ✤
More thrilling adventures with Samantha!

Clue in the Castle Tower
Samantha's visiting a grand English manor—haunted by a ghost!

The Cry of the Loon
A series of strange accidents at Piney Point has Samantha worried.

The Curse of Ravenscourt
Samantha has a new home—and it's putting everyone in danger!

The Stolen Sapphire
Samantha realizes that someone on her steamship is a jewel thief.

The Lilac Tunnel

My Journey with Samantha

Meet Samantha and take a journey back in time
in a book that lets *you* decide what happens.

There's a knock on the bedroom door. I figure it's my new stepsister, Gracie, who's been coming in and out all morning. It's her room, too, so I *have* to let her in. With a sigh, I roll off the bed and open the door. I'm surprised to see not Gracie, but my stepmom.

She glances at the suitcase on the bed behind me. "Need help unpacking?"

I shake my head. I'm spending the summer here in Plattsburg, New York, with my dad, his new wife, and her daughter, Gracie. I've been here for only a day and a half, but I'm already counting down the days till I can go back to my mom's house in New York City. It's funny—I just moved into a house full of people, but somehow I still feel as if I'm all on my own.

I miss my best friend and neighbor, Stella. I miss my own room and my cat, Maggie. I miss pulling out my laptop and my cell phone whenever I want since Dad says I can use them for only an hour a day. Most of all, I miss my mom. She thought I should spend some time with my dad to get to know his new family, but I miss my *old* family—the way things were a couple of years ago when my mom and dad were still together. Why can't things just go back to the way they were?

My stepmom comes into the room and sees the jewelry I've laid out on the dresser. She "oohs" and "aahs" over a friendship bracelet that Stella made for me before I left home. I can tell that my stepmom is trying to be nice, but I'm just not in the mood for conversation.

"I have something that I think you might like," she says, her eyes hopeful. "I'll be right back."

As my stepmom leaves the room, five-year-old Gracie pokes her face through the doorway. "What're you doing?" she asks.

"Nothing," I mumble. Gracie has been glued to me ever since I got here. It's hard enough to share a room—complete with twin beds and pink princess bedspreads—but Gracie wants to share every waking *moment* with me.

I busy myself organizing the jewelry on my dresser. I reach for Stella's friendship bracelet and quickly slide it into my pocket, afraid that Gracie is going to see it and want to share that, too.

When my stepmom comes back, she dangles something in front of me. It's a necklace—a silver heart pendant on a chain. The pendant must be a hundred years old, and it's not my style at all. I try not to make a face.

"My grandma gave me this when I was about your age," my stepmom says. "It helped me through a pretty tough time. Try it on and see if you like it."

She places the pendant in my hand and squeezes my shoulder. "Gracie and I are going to do some scrapbooking," she says. "Do you want to join us?"

"Um, not right now," I say, trying not to sound rude.

I catch the flicker of disappointment in my stepmom's eyes. "Maybe later," she says, closing the door gently behind her.

As quiet settles over the room, I check the clock. 3:52. I wonder what Stella's doing right now.

I sigh, stretch out on the bed, and examine the pendant. It has a hinge along the left side of the heart. Is it a locket? I slide my thumbnail down the groove on the other side and try to open it, but it won't budge.

I reach for a nail file and try to pry the locket open. Just as I'm about to give up, I hear a *pop*. The now-open locket springs from my hand and disappears over the edge of the bed.

Scooting forward on my stomach, I peer over the side of the bed and reach for the locket. It's empty— no photos, no secret messages, no nothing. But as my fingers close around the locket, I feel my stomach drop. Something shifts beneath me, and then I'm falling. I squeeze my eyes shut, bracing for impact. I wait—one second, two, three—much too long for such a short fall. When my body finally hits the floor, I feel a sharp pain in my temple. *Ouch!* Did I hit the dresser?

As I reach for my forehead, my hand brushes against something rough—not carpet, but something strangely familiar: *grass*. I open my eyes to a field of green, blinking against the blinding sunlight.

My temple is throbbing as I try to sit up. The world spins slowly around me in a colorful haze. I take a deep, steadying breath, a breath filled with the scent of lilacs. I glance over my shoulder at a long row of green bushes bursting with purple flowers. I'm sitting beside a lilac hedge on a broad lawn. Behind me, a tunnel through the hedge leads to another yard. Across the lawn is the back of an enormous gray house, several stories tall with a tower on top.

Suddenly I hear the *creak* of a door hinge and voices. I crawl forward through the tunnel and peer through the leaves at the gray house. A sour-faced woman steps onto the porch. She's wearing a long, old-fashioned skirt and apron, and her brown hair is pulled back into a tight little bun. Behind her, a dark-haired girl skips out onto the porch and down the steps into the backyard. When I see what she's wearing, I suck in my breath. Her fancy pink dress has delicate lace trim, and her wide sash is tied in an enormous bow. These two seem to have walked straight out of the pages of a history book.

As the girl takes a few steps into the yard, my heart races. She's walking right toward me. I shrink back into the tunnel, not sure if I want her to see me or not.

The dark-haired girl perches on the edge of a wooden swing hanging from a tree branch. She can't be more than three feet away. She looks friendly and curious, her brown eyes shining. *Who is she?* I wonder. *Why is she dressed like that?* She looks like someone I'd like to meet, someone with an interesting story to tell.

"Mind you keep your dress tidy, Miss Samantha," the woman calls from the porch.

Now I know the girl's name: *Samantha.*

Suddenly, there's a sharp tug on my foot. Some-one—or some *thing*—is trying to pull me backward into the tunnel!

I yelp, yank my foot away, and scramble out of the hedge. I whirl around to get a good look at my attacker—a redheaded boy with a snub-nosed face. He's on his hands and knees, peering through the tunnel from the yard next door.

"Hey!" he says in an accusatory tone. "What were you doing in there?"

About the Author

VALERIE TRIPP says that she became a writer because of the kind of person she is. She says she's curious, and writing requires you to be interested in everything. Talking is her favorite sport, and writing is a way of talking on paper. She's a daydreamer, which helps her come up with her ideas. And she loves words. She even loves the struggle to come up with just the right words as she writes and rewrites. Ms. Tripp lives in Maryland with her husband.